# THE COCAINE PRINCESS 4

King Rio

**Lock Down Publications and Ca$h
Presents**

# The Cocaine Princess 4

**A Novel by *King Rio***

King Rio

**Lock Down Publications**
P.O. Box 944
Stockbridge, Ga 30281
www.lockdownpublications.com

Copyright 2022 by King Rio
The Cocaine Princess 4

**Lock Down Publications**
**Like our page on Facebook: Lock Down Publications @**
**www.facebook.com/lockdownpublications.ldp**
Book interior design by: **Shawn Walker**

## Stay Connected with Us!

Text **LOCKDOWN** to 22828 to stay up-to-date with new releases, sneak peaks, contests and more…

Thank you!

## Submission Guideline.

Submit the first three chapters of your completed manuscript to ldpsubmissions@gmail.com, subject line: Your book's title. The manuscript must be in a .doc file and sent as an attachment. Document should be in Times New Roman, double spaced and in size 12 font. Also, provide your synopsis and full contact information. If sending multiple submissions, they must each be in a separate email.

Have a story but no way to send it electronically? You can still submit to LDP/Ca$h Presents. Send in the first three chapters, written or typed, of your completed manuscript to:

LDP: Submissions Dept
P.O. Box 944
Stockbridge, Ga 30281

*DO NOT send original manuscript. Must be a duplicate.*

Provide your synopsis and a cover letter containing your full contact information.

Thanks for considering LDP and Ca$h Presents.

## *Dedication*

To the memory of Angela Rabotte.

King Rio

## *Prologue*

The inside of the small church was nearly as frigid as the weather was outside, and the ceiling light fixtures were terribly bright. The new- looking wooden pews were draped in red cloth. A darker shade of red carpeting ran from the door to the choir stage at the rear of the church.

Rita Mae Bishop was on stage. She was naked, and the nails Jenny Costilla had hammered through Rita's hands and ankles held her to the eight-foot wooden cross that stood on the stage. A crown of barbed wire encircled the top of her head. Blood was dripping profusely from her head, hands, and feet. The pain was excruciating, but she could not scream with the strip of duct tape covering her mouth; instead, her would-be screams were agonizing moans, trapped in her throat like an unchewed steak.

"What are you crying for? Huh?" Jenny Costilla snapped. She was standing at the foot of the cross with her hands on the hips of her expensive black dress. Her eyes – gelid, soulless, and unforgiving – were cast up at Rita's trembling body. "I thought you loved Jesus. All I've ever heard you talk about is Jesus Christ. Well now you're just like Him, you fucking religious nut. Let's see God get you out of this little jam."

Jenny turned her back to her crucified hostage and studied the three Mexican cartel thugs flanking the church's front door. The trio of brawny men had held Rita to the cross while Jenny hammered in the nails. They were Miguel, Jenny's younger lover, and two of his friends, who were, like him, former members of the Zeta Cartel. They had assault rifles in their hands; and Jenny knew they would use them without hesitation.

Suddenly, there came a knock at the door. Jenny clasped her hands together and smiled. *Showtime...*

*****

Mercedes Costilla entered the church with tears in her eyes and pain in her heart. The father of her two children had just been killed in Chicago, she'd just seen her father die in her sister Alexus' arms, and now she had to deal with her psychotic Aunt Jenny.

Her mouth fell open at the sight of Alexus' mother on the cross.

Jenny frowned, squinting. Then she spoke in a questioning tone, "Where is Alexus, and where is Papi?"

"Oh my God, are you crazy?!" Mercedes was horrified. She raised a hand to her gaping mouth and her eye became saucers. Miguel shut the door and nudged her in the lower back with his AR-15. Mercedes stumbled forward, unable to look away from Rita on the cross. She'd been freezing cold seconds prior, but now she felt nothing but fear.

Jenny's frown turned into a scowl. "I'll ask you again," she said, picking up a long-barreled shotgun from the front pew and aiming it at her brother's daughter. "Alexus was supposed to bring you, Papi, and Enrique. Now, where are they?"

"Enrique's... in the limo. Papi and Alexus were just shot at T-Walk's club. I was fighting with Blake about him getting my kids' father killed. Then T-Walk came out and started fighting Blake too. I broke a bottle over Blake's head right when he was getting ready to shoot T-Walk, and the gun went off. It hit Alexus in the neck and Papi in the chest. I think both of them are dead."

Mercedes was surprised at how quickly the lie had spilled from her mouth. Juan "Papi" Costilla had truly been accidentally shot by Blake, but Alexus was fine. She was outside in her Rolls Royce limousine with Enrique, her chief of security.

The lie was part of the plan to get Rita back without getting everyone else killed. Mercedes hoped and prayed it would work.

Slowly, Jenny lowered the shotgun, and just as slowly, Mercedes lowered her eyes from the cross to Aunt Jenny.

"No," Jenny said. "That can't be."

"It's true, Aunt Jenny. Alexus and Papi are dead. If you kill Rita, Costilla Corp. will be owned by Rita's family. We'll lose billions. Please, get her down from that cross. Why would you do something like this?"

Jenny began pacing a tight circle in front of the cross, gazing down at the crimson carpet and thinking. If Juan and Alexus were dead, Mercedes was probably right. The billions of dollars the Costilla Cartel had worked so many years to accumulate would undoubtedly be lost to a family full of black Americans, and Jenny

10

could not allow that to happen. She'd intended on forcing Papi and Alexus to hand over leadership of the family cartel to her, using Rita as leverage. Now that that option was obviously moot, she had to come up with something else.

She stopped pacing and regarded Mercedes with a malevolent grin, a grin so terrifyingly evil that it could only belong to America's most- wanted fugitive.

Jenny had stolen a bunch of Highly Enriched Uranium from Germany, and the FBI was after her for it. She's already been arrested, jailed in the Guantanamo Bay military prison, and acquitted for her alleged ties to al-Qaeda. Now the American government suspected her of stealing the HEU to build a nuclear weapon.

Unbeknownst to them, she'd already done it.

"You know something, Mercedes," Jenny said, still grinning as she grabbed her briefcase from a front pew and headed up the aisle toward her beautiful nineteen-year-old niece. "I really hadn't thought this whole thing through. Rita might have a will leaving all the money to her family, or to that rapper son-in-law of hers. I hadn't considered that. Killing her could bring down our cartel, and the Zeta and Sinaloa cartels would take over all of Mexico. I can't let that happen." She stopped in front of Mercedes and handed Miguel the briefcase. "Open that for me, will you? Give me that phone out of there."

"Please," Mercedes begged, "don't hurt anyone else. Just leave, Aunt Jenny. Go back to Mexico. Let Rita live."

Jenny's diabolic grin widened. "You'd better not be lying about Papi and Alexus getting shot," she said, accepting a Samsung smartphone from Miguel. She dialed a number, waited a few seconds, and then ended the call and stared into her niece's frightened green eyes. "I'll find out if you're lying."

"I'm not lying, Aunt Jenny. I swear," Mercedes lied.

"Doesn't really matter if you are. I'll be the boss of the Costil-la Cartel one of these days, you wait and see. All those billions will be *mine*. They cut me out of the family business! After all I've sacrificed, they pushed me out of the cartel and let in a bunch of Americans! Well, you know what?" Jenny moved closer to Mercedes, so close that their noses almost touched.

Mercedes shivered in fear.

"Tonight," Jenny hissed, "I will bring America to its knees. Your miserable little country is going to pay for the torture I endured in that filthy military prison. If Alexus and Papi are dead, then that means my brother Flako will be running things from now on; and after tonight, he'll be the sole cartel boss in Mexico. America will fall, and the Costilla Cartel will rise to new heights, heights that Escobar could have only dreamed of reaching. And seizing power from Flako will be a piece of cake.

Jenny showed another grin, then pulled open the door and led her goons outside.

*****

From behind the darkly tinted side windows of her long white Phantom limo, Alexus watched as Aunt Jenny exited the church with three armed men and crossed the street to a black Audi sedan.

'God, please let my mom be okay,' Alexus prayed tearfully, squeezing her eyes tightly. When she opened them a moment later, Mercedes was standing at her door with Reesie Cup, who had followed them there in his dark colored Bentley. Mercedes got in next to her, and Cup stuck his bald brown head in the open door.

"I called the police," Mercedes mumbled. "They should be here with an ambulance in a few minutes. Rita's hurt pretty badly. Hopefully, she'll make it through alright."

Cup chimed in, "Blake and T-Walk are being rushed to the hospital as we speak. They shot each other right after we left the club. Alexus, you and I need to talk business."

"Now is not the time, Cup," Mercedes snapped.

"I understand you all have a lot going on, but as you know, my stash house in Chicago was just raided. I need at least two or three hundred bricks to keep things flowing in my city."

Mercedes sucked her teeth indignantly and ignored Cup's selfish request.

"What did that lunatic do to my mother?" Alexus asked her sister. "You don't wanna know. Trust me; you do not want to know."

Another double stream of tears rolled down Alexus' face. Her heart was throbbing sporadically in her chest, and her blood-

12

stained hands – stained with the blood of her father, who'd died in her arms less than twenty minutes ago – were buried in the deep pockets of her equally bloodied white fur coat, trembling.

*'What would Papi do?'* she asked herself, gazing vacantly at the twelve-bottle case of *Ace of Spades* champagne on the floor across from her. *'Papi wouldn't be sitting here like I am, crying my eyes out and shaking in my Louboutins.'*

Gradually, the tears attenuated. Her heart stopped thumping so rapidly in her chest. Alexus was now the boss of the Costilla Cartel; she had to start acting like it.

Wiping away the tears with the sleeve of her coat, Alexus moved to the other side of the thirteen passenger limo. She knocked on the black window separating the driver's cabin from the rear passenger's cabin. It slid down an inch.

"Enrique," Alexus said, her tone resolute, "Soon an ambulance will be here for my mom. Follow it to the hospital."

The window slid shut.

"Get in, Cup," Alexus said. "We're safe in here. The whole thing's bullet-proof and bomb-resistant."

A part of Alexus wanted badly to go inside the church and check on her mother, but with Aunt Jenny in the picture, she deemed it best to sit in the armored limo until either the Michigan City Police Department or her security team arrived.

Cup got in beside Mercedes, who quickly scooted over to her sister's side before Cup had even closed the door.

Alexus pressed a button that locked all of the doors.

"What happened with your mom?" Cup asked, adjusting his pinstriped Armani suit jacket.

Rocking back and forth in her seat, Alexus ignored Cup and stared out her window at the white clapboarded side of the church. Her mind wandered. Her hands clenched and unclenched in her pockets.

Her phone began vibrating against the gold-plated .44 revolver in her left pocket. She pulled the iPhone out, saw that it was Enrique calling, and answered it.

Just then, a fleet of seven snow-white Chevy SUVs appeared from every direction, and police sirens screamed in the distance.

The Tahoes were occupied by Alexus' bodyguards, an elite team of heavily armed gunmen.

"We should leave before the cops get here," Enrique advised. "We can wait at the hospital, but sticking around here after what just happened at the nightclub could spell disaster for us all. I'll have four vehicles stay behind to look after Rita."

Alexus sighed. She knew that Enrique was right. Lingering around police after she'd just shot two guys at the club would be a foolish mistake.

Reluctantly, she agreed to leave, and Enrique sped off down Willard Avenue. They zipped past a group of dark-clothed black teens on the corner of Patrick Street. More hustlers stood outside Bee Kay's convenience store on 9th Street. Alexus gazed out the window across from her until they turned onto a deserted back road behind Indiana State Prison.

Then her attention shifted to Cup. He spoke first.

"I apologize for pressing you for dope at a time like this. I saw the whole fight between T-Walk and Blake. If Mercedes hadn't jumped in and hit Blake with that bottle, he wouldn't have accidentally shot your pops. He was trying to shoot T-Walk."

"Fuck Blake!" Mercedes snapped. "That motherfucker just had the father of my kids *killed*. I hope T-Walk blew his fucking head off." Combing her fingers through her hair, she turned to her half-sister with an unforgiving scowl. "I wish I'd never met you, Alexus. You got my mom killed and now your ex is responsible for the death of my kids' father.

You're lucky I'm not kicking your ass al through this limousine right now. Dirty bitch."

Mercedes was opening her mouth to vent some more when Alexus whipped the revolver out of her coat pocket. Mercedes gasped at the sight of it.

Alexus pointed the gun at Cup's chest. His eyes widened.

"Think we don't know that it was you who kidnapped Blake's daughter? Huh? You kidnapped my precious little step-daughter, forced us to pay fifty million of my money to get her back, and now you want a favor?" Alexus shook her head. "Nuh-uh. It doesn't work like that."

Cup was rushing to unlock his door when the first deafening gunshot struck his chest, and he caught three more rounds in the side of his gaudy suit jacket as he pushed open the door and leapt out into the darkness. Alexus moved to shut the door and watched him tumble along the grassy roadside.

"Lexi, what's wrong with you?!" Mercedes shouted.

Pulling the door shut, Alexus turned the gun on her sister. "Listen: I know I had your mom killed, but I told you it wasn't on purpose. If you think you're going to kill me or harm me about it, you're sadly mistaken.

I'll leave you on the side of this road with Cup."

A frigid expression grew on Mercedes' pretty face. She glowered at Alexus through stringently squinted eyelids. "You're pointing a gun at me?" she muttered in disbelief.

"I'll do more than point it."

"You're going crazy, Alexus, just like Papi and Jenny and that crazy nigga Blake."

"I'm not crazy," Alexus stated coldly. "But I'll act like it if I need

to."

Mercedes shook her head incredulously, and the rode to St. Anthony's Hospital in silence.

\*\*\*\*\*

Rita Mae Bishop was already being rushed into the ER on a stretcher when Enrique jerked the limo to a stop near the emergency room's sliding glass doors. The paramedics had sawed through the cross to remove Rita from it, leaving the nails in her hands and ankles with square blocks of wood behind them.

Alexus, Enrique, and a phalanx of bodyguards followed the stretcher into the emergency room. Mercedes stayed in the limo.

Seeing her mother's blood dripping profusely from the side of the stretcher sent Alexus into an even deeper state of shock than the one she had experienced outside the church.

The ER was packed full of Blake and T-Walk's family and friends. After Rita was wheeled through a pair of wooden doors, Alexus found an empty seat beside a thuggishly dressed dark-skinned man with thick braids and sat down. The guy introduced

15

himself as Rico G and said he was there for Blake; but Alexus ignored him and stared blankly at the tiled floor. She didn't want to talk to anyone. The three people she loved most in life – Momma, Blake, and T-Walk – were fighting for their lives somewhere inside this hospital, and she was holding herself responsible for their injuries. Tears sprang forth from her verdant green eyes.

Enrique slapped a mammoth paw onto Alexus' shoulder and gave it a gentle rub. His broken, bleeding nose and badly swollen face were clear reminders of the beating he'd taken from one of T-Walk's goons a short while ago.

He lowered his mouth to her ear and whispered, "I'm heading back there to get my face checked out." Enrique gave Alexus' shoulder a firm squeeze. "Be strong, Alexus, for the family and the family business. You're running the show now. Billions of dollars are at stake. You must become twice as fierce as you Aunt Jenny, ten times as cunning as Papi, and just as wise as your grandmother was if you want to live in peace. Sit tight. I'll see if I can find out how Blake and T-Walk are doing while I'm getting looked at." He patted her shoulder, then left to seek medical attention.

Alexus' eyes never strayed from the floor. She heard people murmuring all around her.

"Isn't that Bulletface's girlfriend?" someone nearby muttered. "That's Alexus Costilla, the billionaire," said another voice.

Alexus tuned them out and kept her eyes on the floor. The notion of suicide flitted across her mind. Anything was better than living in the same world with her perilous aunt.

There was a wide-screen television in the corner across the room from her. It was on CNN. Wolf Blitzer was solemnly reminding America of the tragedies surrounding the country's wealthiest woman. He spoke of the multiple murders at MTN Tower, headquarters of Alexus' television Network in downtown Chicago. He shared the breaking news of the Blake King and Trintino Walkson shooting and reported that both men were listed in critical condition at a northwest Indiana hospital.

Then came the most daunting news of all.

The White House had just announced the United States was on high alert for potential terrorist attacks. Chicago was on lockdown. Military troops were out in full force, searching for Jennifer

Costilla, the FBI's most wanted fugitive, who was suspected of smuggling nuclear material – possibly a nuclear weapon – into the country. CNN viewers were just seconds away from an Oval Office speech, to be delivered by the president himself. U.S. citizens were immersed in a boiling pot of fear and speculation, and at the center of it all was Alexus Costilla.

She'd been seated close to thirty minutes when a pair of aging white sneakers appeared on the spot of the floor she was staring so vacantly at.

She looked up and found a thin man wearing a shirt and tie with a white lab jacket over it. An ID tag hanging from the front left pocket identified him as Dr. Streeter. He was pale-faced with round glasses and a gray beard, and he had a clipboard in his hand.

Alexus took a deep breath and prepared for the worst.

"Ms. Costilla, am I right?" he asked, flipping up a page on the clipboard.

Reluctantly, Alexus nodded.

I have you listed here as the primary contact for Blake King, and secondary contact for Trintino Walkson. They're in surgery now. Walkson was shot in the left arm, and another bullet tore through his upper right shoulder. King was shot in the face and neck. God must have been watching over him tonight, because the bullet that entered his right cheek went around his skull and out the back, instead of straight through. The hole in the side of his neck is a half of an inch away from his jugular vein. He's lucky to be alive. Cases like his are rare." Dr. Streeter licked his thumb and flipped another page. "Your mom has lost a lot of blood, but she'll live, as will King and Walkson. Some FBI guys just came in asking to speak with you. I can hold them off if you'd like to wait a—"

A collective gasp suddenly swept across the room.

All eyes settled on the television, and for a while no one said a word. They were watching live video of a massive mushroom of fire that seemed to stretch for miles in every direction. Through tearful eyes and an emotionally torn voice, Wolf presented the breaking news.

"Ladies and gentlemen, it breaks my heart to inform you that nuclear weapons have reportedly been detonated in Mazatlán and Juarez, Mexico, and right here in our very own backyard. Washington, D.C. has been nuked. Our nation's capital stands no more. The White House is down. I repeat, the White House is down."

## *Chapter 1*
## *One Year Later*

So, has life been treating you better? Have you spoken to your son's father since our last session?"

"No."

"No, life hasn't been treating you any better; or no, you haven't heard from your son's father?"

"Both. My life sucks, and Blake's still mad at me for cheating on him with T-Walk."

Alexus let out a frustrated breath. She was lying on the dark leather sofa across the office from Melonie Farr, the psychologist/relationship specialist she'd been seeing every Friday for the past two months.

It was a sparsely decorated office. A few framed certificates hung on the walls. There was a small table next to the door, atop which a glass vase full of white flowers stood. There was also a big oak desk where Farr was always seated, jotting down notes and gazing thoughtfully at Alexus.

Brown-skinned and diminutive with an ever-present smile and lively hazel eyes, Farr was a Harvard graduate with a recently opened office in downtown Chicago. The wealthiest of Chicagoans brought their problems to her, and since Rita Mae Bishop was already visiting the bland office twice a week, Alexus had decided to join the crowd.

"Correct me if I'm wrong, Alexus. I believe you did more than cheat. You *left* Blake for T-Walk. That's a lot worse than cheating."

"I didn't leave him. He caught me cheating and left me."

"But you didn't try to make it right. You were engaged to that man; and when he caught you cheating, you made the decision to stay with the guy you were cheating with. Now, since T-Walk has cheated on you, you want Blake back. He has a right to be upset. I'd be just as upset, if not more."

Pinching the white diamond tennis bracelet on her wrist, Alexus gritted her teeth in frustration. "I know. I'm dumb."

"No, you're not dumb. You're a young woman, and like most young women, you make mistakes. Dwelling on it will get you nowhere. If you want Blake back in your life, you have to show him. Tell him how much he means to you. Tell him how much you miss him and want him. You messed up your relationship so it's your responsibility to fix it, or at least try to. You owe it to your son."

Farr was right, and Alexus knew it. She screwed up royally, shattered her love life completely, and it was on her to pick up the pieces and put them back together.

"Are the feds still hounding you about your aunt?" Farr asked.

Alexus didn't get a chance to reply. At that very moment, Enrique barged into the office with a serious look on his face.

"We've got trouble," he said, and Alexus shivered.

## *Chapter 2*

The most wanted terrorist in human history—accused of killing over four hundred thousand Americans and an equal number of Mexican citizens in last year's attacks—stood silently between the three bound captives kneeled in front of her and the twenty heavily armed men behind her. The cartel thugs wore camouflage uniforms, bulletproof vests, and black masks that covered their entire faces, but Jennifer Costilla was bare-faced, clad in a black Valentino dress and Manolo Blahnic flats. She had a razor-sharp hunting knife in hand. Ten feet ahead of her was a camcorder on a tripod, and her cold eyes were glued to it.

They were in a remote jungle of southern Venezuela, but the large black curtain erected behind them would conceal their location from the many government agencies that were already searching far and wide for the woman they'd labeled "Public Enemy Number One."

A bird chirped from a treetop nearby. Jenny was hot and sweaty, and she was getting upset about it. The masked man behind the camera was taking too long to get it working. One of the three men kneeled before Jenny had started sobbing and mumbling a prayer a few minutes prior, and this too irritated Jenny.

*'I killed the president of the United States last year,'* Jenny thought to herself, *'but I can't get this guy to properly use a camera.'* She grunted and squinted and exhaled sharply, wondering if Alexus had yet to learn of the suicide bombing at the Costilla's restaurant in Matamoros, Mexico.

Finally, the man behind the camera nodded his head. "Are we live?" Jenny asked.

He nodded again.

Jenny stared into the camera lens without speaking for nearly a full minute. Then, after checking to make sure the hands of her captives were securely tied behind their backs, she grabbed a handful of the crying man's hair and opened his throat with her knife. He struggled against his restraints until he was too weak to struggle any longer. Jenny continued to saw through his neck, enjoying the feel of his warm blood on her hand. She let go of his hair, moved over to the second captive, and slit his throat while her ruthless young lover, Miguel, severed the crybaby's head with three powerful swings of a long-handled ax. They repeated the grisly process until all three captives were headless and twitching on the narrow dirt road.

Jenny picked up one of the heads by the hair at the top of its scalp, stared briefly into its vapid green eyes, and pressed her lips against its forehead. It was her nephew, Antoney Costilla's head, her brother Flako's son.

Miguel lifted the other two heads and showed them to the camera, and Jenny did the same with Antoney's head.

"Let this be a message to the boss of the Matamoros Cartel," Jenny said while carving out Antoney's left eyeball. "Give me the ten. All I want is the ten. Give them to me and, on my mother's grave, I'll never be heard from again. *Don't* give them to me and... well, you know. You remember. I blew half of Mexico and Washington, D.C. to the moon, didn't I? I've got enough plutonium and uranium left to do it twice more. So have the ten at the place where the Omnipotent stands in four days, or I'm doing it again."

She tossed her nephew's head aside, stabbed the tip of her knife into the back of the gelatinous eyeball, and pointed it at the camera.

"See you soon," she said with a wicked grin.

22

## *Chapter 3*

"There's been a suicide bombing at your restaurant in Matamoros, and Antoney's gone missing." Enrique was leaning over Alexus as she lay supine on the sofa, trying vehemently to remain calm, to think like a drug- lord and not like a twenty-one-year-old Texas girl.

Melonie Farr stood up behind her desk and folded her arms over her chest, but she didn't interrupt Enrique's whispers.

"Now," he went on, "we know that the Zeta and the Sinaloa Cartels are practically extinct, so I'm guessing the attack came from elsewhere.

And we both know that it could not have been the Gulf Cartel."

"Aunt Jenny," Alexus murmured knowingly.

"That was my guess, too." "Where's my uncle?"

"Flako's already on a plane to Matamoros. He's worried sick.

Antoney was supposed to have a meeting with those Dominicans in New York City, but he never showed, and he isn't answering his phone. Bella and Pedro haven't heard from him either."

Alexus sighed and pinched the bridge of her nose. "Bring out a thousand armed men in Matamoros. I want everyone questioned. Somebody had to have seen something. And make sure my mom is—"

"Your mother is safe. We've got close to fifty armed guards at the MTN Tower."

"Well, double check. And make sure Mercedes, Tasia, and Cereniti have around-the-clock security as well. Give me a few more minutes with Farr and I'll be right out."

As Enrique was turning to leave, Farr said, "You may want to stay a bit longer Alexus. We've hardly covered one issue. And what was that all about? Does it have anything to do with your aunt?"

Sitting up, Alexus locked eyes with the psychologist but said nothing. It was a silent answer.

"What else do we need to discuss this week?" Farr walked over to the door and closed it. "We need a solution to the tension between you and your sister. I truly meant to bring that up first. Have you talked to Mercedes?"

No. She got married to Kenny a couple of weeks ago. I saw the wedding pics on Instagram. The itch didn't even send me an invite. It's okay, because as soon as she runs through that petty little change I gave her, she'll come begging for some more money, and I'm not giving her a dime. That forty million is all the money she'll ever get from me."

"Forty million *dollars*?" Farr scoffed and sat back down in her swivel chair. "Jesus Christ, that is a lot of money. She'll never go broke."

"Yes she will. She's already burned through over half of it." Alexus stood up, nervously flicking her eyes from the door to the small window on the other side of the office as if at any moment Aunt Jenny would burst through one of the two. "Listen, Farr, I really have to—"

"I told you, call me Mel or Melonie."

"Okay, well… Melonie, I've really got to get going. There's a lot going on right now, and I have to deal with it all personally." Alexus took a contemplative pause. "There's been a suicide bombing at my restaurant in Mexico. That's about all I can say for now."

"I'd sit down and finish this session if I were you." "And why is that?" Alexus inquired, grabbing her hips. Just then, the office door swung open again.

This time it was not Enrique.

Alexus gasped in shock and her heart inflated in her chest.

## *Chapter 4*

He wore an all-black Versace ensemble: a thick hoody, loose-fitting leather jogging pants with bundles of hundred-dollar bills peeking halfway out its side pockets. A skullcap canted to the left of his head, exposing the perfect waves of hair on the other side. A chunky rope of braided gold hung from his neck, attached to it was a large gold pendant depicting a money bag with MBM written across it in gleaming yellow diamonds. Ten-carat cubes of yellow ice sparkled in his pinkie rings and earrings. Diamonds of the same color encircled the gold watch on his left wrist.

He smiled a mouthful of diamond-encrusted platinum teeth at his beautiful ex-fiancée and walked to her with his arms open for a hug.

Tears grew in Alexus' eyes, and when Blake "Bulletface" King stopped before her, she too was smiling.

She raised a hand from her hip and slapped him hard across the face.

Then she put her forehead on his shoulder, wrapped her arms around him, and squeezed with all her might. "I hate you so much," she cried. But Blake knew she didn't mean it; so he pulled her closer and rubbed his hands up and down her back for a moment.

"Awwwww, that's sweet," Melonie cooed as she crossed the room to shut the door behind Blake. She was back in her chair an instant later, arms folded, smiling from ear to ear.

"Explain to me what's sweet about me getting slapped," Blake said with an equally wide smile. "Is this why you called me here? So I could get abused by this crazy ass woman?"

Giggling softly, Alexus unglued her face from his shoulder, looked him in the eyes, and pecked her soft lips against his. "Shut up, Blake. Ain't nobody abusing you." She gave him a second kiss and they sat next to each other on the sofa. "I was just surprised, that's all. Mel didn't tell me you were coming." She squeezed his right hand in her left hand and delivered yet another kiss to his cheek, and suddenly all three of them were smiling broadly.

"I can't be long," Blake said. "Got a studio session with Yeezy starting in a few hours."

"Well," Melonie looked at Alexus, "Let's get to it."

25

Alexus took a deep breath and turned to Blake. Emotions bounced around in her chest and brought more tears to her eyes. She quickly wiped them away.

"I'm sorry, Blake," she began. "I'm sorry for cheating on you with T-Walk and staying with him afterwards. I'm sorry for sending you those fake DNA test results saying King Neal was T-Walk's. I'm sorry for everything, okay? Please find it in your heart to forgive me. I miss you, Blake. I miss you and I love you and I need you. I don't want to be a single mom; and I certainly don't want another man playing the role of my son's father. You're the only..." Alexus' voice cracked. She sniffled twice, and then broke down crying again.

Blake pulled her head to his chest. "Don't cry, baby," he said, amorously caressing her shoulder. "We both messed up. But we got each other now. That's all that matters."

## *Chapter 5*

After helping Alexus into her full-length white leather coat and planting a reassuring kiss on the nape of her neck, Blake led the way out of the North Rush Street office building, followed by Enrique and four more burly Mexican men in black suits.

A dozen identically dressed bodyguards flanked the four white SUVs that were parked behind Alexus' snow-white Maybach. Blake's armored Bugatti Veyron sports car—matte black and tinted and clean as a whistle—was parked across the street in front of his friend and fellow rapper, Young D's black BMW X6.

"I know I've got a lot of explaining to do," Alexus said. "I have a penthouse at the Trump. It's right around the corner from here. We can talk there."

"A'ight, but I can't be long. Got Kanye working on my album with me, and you know how he is. And I still got verses to record for this mixtape I'm dropping next week."

The two of them were standing chest to chest, almost nose to nose. Blake put his hands on her ass and cursed the coat for being in the way. He missed having Alexus so close. Gazing into her gentle green eyes, impervious to the icy daggers of winter air that were stabbing through his hoody, he tapped his lips against hers and made a pledge to himself to keep her for good this time.

"Can't I just go to the studio with you? I don't want to leave you so soon," Alexus whined.

"I don't want you to leave, either," Blake replied. And just like that, their love was rekindled.

The 14,000-square-foot penthouse on the 89th floor of the Trump belonged to Alexus Costilla. She had purchased it for $30 million, then spent another $22 million bringing it up to designer-magazine quality. The penthouse rambled over the top two floors and looked out from its many large windows at Lake Michigan. The overhead included a chef, a butler, two maids, a valet, a babysitter, and Tasia Olsen, Alexus' best friend and personal assistant.

Following Enrique and Alexus inside, Blake's eyes rolled around in their sockets as he took in the lavish penthouse's all-white décor. There were white marble floors and countertops, white leather sofas and easy chairs. White-framed portraits of Alexus' family members lined the walls. As Alexus was leading Blake into a spacious bedroom, two-year-old King Neal Costilla came speeding out of a room further down the hall in a miniature white Mercedes Maybach. His face lit up when he saw Blake. He hopped out of the car and wrapped his arms around Blake's leg. Like Alexus, he was wearing white jeans and a white shirt, and he resembled Blake so much that now there could be no questioning his paternity.

"What's up lil homie?" Blake said, rubbing his son's head and entering the bedroom with King—or King Neal, as the media was fond of calling him—still clinging to his leg.

"Daddy, why you never come see me no more?" King Neal let go of the leg and crossed his arms over his chest as Blake and Alexus settled into the big leather sofa that sat at the foot of the bed. His smile was dim and there were tears in his eyes, which were green like his mother's. "My momma said she did somethin' mean to you and that's why you didn't come over no more."

"I did, King," said Alexus as she kicked off her white leather boots and folded her legs beneath her. She too was teary eyed. "Mommy messed up, okay? Mommy messed up big time. It's not your dad's fault."

King Neal turned his head from left to right. "*I* didn't make you mad, Daddy. *You* made *me* mad because you stopped coming to see me!"

Blake lifted his son onto his knee. The little guy put his head down and kept his arms crossed. It broke Blake's heart to know that he'd hurt his son's feelings. He had been meaning to mend the issues he had with Alexus for a while now, but his schedule over the past year had been hectic. As CEO of Money Bagz Management, the record label he started a few years prior, he was always busy going over beats, recording music, working with his artists, and performing all across the country. According to Forbes, his net worth was $712 million, making him the leading figure in hip-hop, and he was trying to stay the lead.

"You're right, King. I shouldn't have punished you for something you didn't do." Blake gave the nape of his son's neck a comforting squeeze, and then slid his hand up to King Neal's head and shook it. "Give me a minute to talk to Alexus, okay? We're about to make sure this never happens again."

"You didn't say 'sorry,' Dad. I want an agopoly. You gotta say it." Alexus and Blake laughed in unison.

"It's called an 'apology,' King, not an 'agopoly,'" Alexus said. Finally, King Neal's smile returned.

"I apologize, King. A'ight? We cool now?" Blake was all smiles.

"Yeah," King Neal said, "as long as you stay this time and never leave again; 'cause I want you and Momma together so my sister can move in with us."

"High-five?" Blake raised his palm and King Neal slapped his little hand into it before hopping down from Blake's knee and running out of the room.

Alexus got up and went to lock the bedroom door, and Blake enjoyed watching her walk. She still possessed an ass that rivaled Tahiry Jose's.

"King reminds me so much of you," she said, stopping and grabbing her hips as Blake kicked off his sneakers and fell across the bed. "Uuuuum... I think I remember saying we were coming here to *talk*, Blake. I didn't say anything about you getting in my bed."

"Shut up. Please. Just come sit on my lap so we can talk face to face." Blake put on his signature grin.

Rolling her eyes and sucking her teeth, Alexus mounted him on the bed and put her hands on his throat as if she wanted to choke him.

"I might miss you, but I certainly don't miss that mouth of yours," she said. "Well... I kinda miss the mouth, too," she added a second later.

Momentarily, the two of them were silent. Blake rubbed his hands up and down her enormous derriere, this time cursing the jeans for being in the way. Alexus traced the scars on his face with her thumbs. Three years ago, two bullets had entered his left cheek, spiraled through his mouth, and exited his right cheek. Just above the two exit wounds was the spot where he'd been shot last year.

"You really ought to stop chasing bullets," Alexus suggested.

"What I need to do is stay the fuck away from you. You're bad luck.

I didn't start gettin' shot until you came along."

Another happy silence ensued. Blake felt like he was in heaven. He wanted this moment to last forever.

"I'm so sorry for what I out you through," Alexus said, lowering her face to his. "Cheating on you was the biggest mistake of my life. I can't take it back, but what I can do is promise to never do it again. I'm going through so much with the family business, and with the television network, and Aunt Jenny. I need someone I can trust to have my back, Blake. You're the only man I love and trust completely. I'll do whatever it takes to have you back in my life."

"I'm here, baby. And I'm here to stay this time." "Promise?"

"I promise. Now get naked."

Alexus giggled and pushed his face to the side. "I see you haven't changed a bit. Nasty ass." She grinded her crotch down against the steel- hard pole in his pants, cradled his handsome brown face in her hands, and softly bit his bottom lip. "Boy, I'm about to ride you to death."

He assisted her in eagerly removing his hoody, as well as the shirt and bullet proof vest he had on under it. His daily weightlifting sessions had his muscles bulging, and Alexus took a moment to admire his herculean physique before she began planting kisses from his neck to his chest and sharply chiseled six-pack.

"I'd give anything to have this body all to myself," she said, then gasped as Blake flipped her over onto her back, pushed up her shirt, and freed her breasts from her white lace bra.

"Anything?" He squeezed her breasts and sucked a nipple into his

mouth.

"Yes, Blake. Anything. *Any*thing," she replied as she hurriedly

unfastened her belt. Just as hurriedly, Blake stripped her of her jeans and white thong panties.

He quickly separated her thighs and gave her clitoris a long, passionate kiss. The delicious scent of her womanhood ignited a fiery hunger within him, and the taste of it made his twelve-inch phallus throb. He tongued and sucked her clitoris, rubbing his

30

hands up and down her winding hips as she held his head and moaned. A few minutes of this was all it took to bring Alexus to a quivering orgasm. She let out a loud moan, and her sweet nectar gushed out onto Blake's steadily slurping lips.

He rose to his knees, smiling as if he'd just conquered the world, and whipped out his long black rod. He was guiding it into her when someone knocked on the bedroom door.

"Lexi, what the hell are you in there doing, yo? I can hear pretty damn good, and it sounds to me like you're doing the most with that damn dildo."

Alexus laughed. "Get away from my door, Tee-Tee."

Slowly, Blake eased his thick muscle into her snug love tunnel. She gasped and dug her fingernails in his strong back.

"Girl, I hope you ain't brought no nigga up in here without introducing him to me and Tasia," said the babysitter, Cereniti "Tee-Tee" Stingley.

Blake sank most of his pole into Alexus in one quick stroke that made her moan and gasp again. Grinning widely at her ecstatic, open- mouthed expression, and at the sound of Cereniti yelling for Tasia and shaking the locked doorknob, Blake started sliding in and out, penetrating her deeply with every inward thrust. Alexus moaned incessantly beneath him. He kissed her lips, her chin, and sucked on her neck and breasts.

"Blake's in there!" Cereniti shouted.

"Mmmm hmmm," came Tasia's voice. "King snitched on you. That's a damn shame. You ain't seen that nigga in a whole year and the first thing you do is give up the pussy."

"Yo, you're mad slutty for that, Lex."

"I know, right? Mad slutty," Tasia agreed.

"We'll be down at the pool when you're done getting your back blown out. You lil freak," Cereniti added with a laugh.

Blake chuckled once and continued pounding in and out of his favorite woman. They changed positions minutes later, and Alexus rode him cow-girl style, mashing her breasts together and biting the corner of her bottom lip as he held onto her wildly undulating ass and enjoyed the ride.

Her seemingly effortless riding skills, combined with her raucous moans and sexy facial expressions, had Blake's semen jetting out of his foot-long pole in no time. Alexus dropped down with all of her weight and rolled her hips as he filled her with his cream.

"Damn," Blake said, his chest rising and falling with every breath.

His grin returned. "Damn, baby. Damn."

"Did I just reduce your vocabulary to those two words?"
"Damn near."

With a beaming smile, Alexus hopped off the bed and sauntered into the adjoining bathroom.

Blake was seconds behind her.

## *Chapter 6*

### FBI Headquarters Quantico, VA

"Jennifer Costilla is Osama bin Laden to the fiftieth power. She's responsible for single-handedly murdering over four hundred thousand Americans, including our former President, First Lady, Vice President, and too many high-ranking government officials to name. She's the reason our stock market crashed and sent this great country into the worst recession in

U.S. history, the reason our new President and First Family are living underground here in Virginia instead of in D.C. where they belong. She's the reason food and gas prices have risen by more than seventy percent! We're the fucking FBI, for Christ's sake! Why have we not been able to locate this lunatic? Why is she not in our custody? Gotdammit I want answers!"

There were close to forty of the FBI's finest seated around the two long conference tables in the center of the room, and all eyes were on FBI Director Charles Byrd, who was spewing his histrionic harangue from in front of a dry-erase board with a large picture of Jennifer Costilla taped to the middle of it.

Short and chubby, with a balding scalp and ever-present cantankerous expression, Director Byrd was a former Navy S.E.A.L. Team Six member with a chest full of medals and a heart full of American pride. He flicked his eyes around the room, searching for answers.

The pale white hand of Josh Sneed, Special Agent in charge of Chicago FBI, rose slowly; he glanced around, saw that his was the only hand raised, and briefly considered lowering it.

"This better be good," boomed Director Byrd.

"Sir," said Sneed, "I believe we aren't looking enough into the Costilla family as a whole. We've overlooked the richest woman in American history. Alexus Costilla is not an innocent bystander in all this. Her father was Juan Costilla, and we all know his drug cartel was in cahoots with the CIA. Who's to say Alexus hasn't taken the throne? It would certainly explain why Jenny's been after her for so long. Maybe Jenny

wants control of the cartel. Maybe, if we can get someone close to Alexus, someone she trusts, she'll reveal Jennifer's

33

location. It's worth a shot, if you ask me."

"No." Byrd shook his head in disagreement. "For one, there is no such thing as a Costilla family drug cartel. DEA says it no longer exists. And secondly, Alexus has been one hundred percent cooperative with this manhunt. There's no way she's going to jeopardize her fifty-billion-dollar empire for a woman who crucified her mother. If Alexus ever finds out where Jennifer's hiding, I'm sure we'll be the first to know."

"What if she already knows? I'm betting she does."

Now all eyes were on Sneed. He stood and cleared his throat, wondering if Byrd was among the thousands of government officials on the Costilla Cartel's payroll. He'd dealt with the Costillas before. They threw their wealth in every direction, and their power was rumored to reach as far as the White House—well, the old White House.

"I was with Alexus in Miami when that plane was hijacked and crashed into her beach house. Then I visited her after a sniper tried to take her out in Chicago. Her life is like an action movie. All her phones have scrambling devices on them, her security detail puts Secret Service to shame, and she's always whispering to her head of security, that Enrique guy. I'm absolutely certain she's hiding *a lot* of secrets. We need to get someone close to her to wire up and start asking questions. I believe that's all it'll take to find Jenny. Since Alexus is notoriously weak when it comes to the men she dates, and since she's currently single, I suggest we send in a love interest and see if she'll fold. Set it up real nice, you know. She's living the American dream, but she has yet to find the love of her dreams. Let's send him to her. She likes good-looking black men, so let's create the perfect candidate. Make him the most irresistible temptation. There aren't many Americans who will turn down the chance to assist us in finding Jenny, so finding a man for the job will be a piece of cake. Our only challenge will be in getting them together."

"What if that big-time TV producer she was with comes back into the picture? Or that rapper?" Byrd inquired.

"This is a matter of national security," said Sneed. "It must be treated as such."

No one commented.

34

They all understood perfectly.

King Rio

## *Chapter 7*

Alexus knocked lightly and entered the dark recording studio with her iPhone 5 in hand. She was skimming through all the major news websites, seeing how many had posted the breaking news of the suicide bombing at her restaurant in Mexico. CNN, ABC, and NBC were already hounding the story. 'Seven dead, thirty injured in Costilla restaurant suicide bombing in northeast Mexico,' CNN reported. She couldn't believe it.

A pall of Kush smoke hung over the room. Blake stood before a microphone in the glassed-in booth with a Styrofoam cup in one hand and a blunt in the other. Kanye was seated at the sound controls. Young D and three other MBM music artists—Meach, Yellow, and Grammy-award- winning R & B singer Mocha—were also present. The male artists were dressed like Blake in black Versace outfits with heavy gold chains, diamond watches, and Styrofoam cups full of Lean (codeine and Sprite). They were nodding their heads to the beat as Blake "Bulletface" King did his thing in the booth. Smiling, Alexus crossed her arms and listened.

*"Got killas wit' me right now and e'rybody know it*
*We got .40 Glocks wit' them thirties and e'rybody blowin' Been shot fourteen times and e'rybody know it*
*Think I'm lettin' it happen again? You got me fucked up, cause nigga I'm blowin'*
*I'm in my black Bugatti wit' that yoppa on me, choppas ain't too far behind me*
*Pussy niggas stay hatin', shit, but they broke and way too far behind me Blackbone in my swimmin' pool, yellowbone in my livin' room*
*Redbone in my bed, I'm hurtin' that pussy into Thanksgivin' soon Opp niggas get shot quicka than sick patients at hospitals*
*These thot bitches be comin' through to suck Bulletface like popsicles Phantom coupes when we roll in, hit my connect now we snowed in We poled up, gun-totin'... diss me and meet yo' end..."*

Alexus' smile widened. She loved Bulletface's music. Just seeing him standing there, with all those teardrop tattoos on his

37

face and those diamonds glistening in his mouth, made Alexus horny all over again. She envisioned them fucking in the recording booth, her legs wrapped tightly around his waist, his throbbing phallus buried deep inside her.

An incoming text message from Tasia shook away the lascivious thoughts. Alexus read the message:

*'Just got off the line with Sprite. Offer raised to $56 mill. Say they're not going any higher.'*

Alexus replied, *'Tell Sprite to kiss my ass. Pepsi gave Beyoncé fifty million! I want DOUBLE!'*

She looked up from the phone as Bulletface opened the booth's glass door and stepped out, sipping his lean and regarding her with dark red eyes. A long 30-round magazine hung out the side of his hoody's belly pocket, clipped into the gun that was bulging out inside the pocket.

He mumbled a few words to Kanye, then passed Young D his half- smoked blunt and led Alexus out to the hallway. They paused just outside the door and gazed lovingly at their children. Savaria, Blake's eight-year- old daughter from a previous relationship, was sitting against the wall next to King Neal, holding a bottle of water to his mouth and watching him drink.

"Don't you just love seeing them together like this?" Alexus rested her arms on Blake's shoulders, keeping her eyes on the kids. "Brother and sister, side by side, I love it."

"He's all she talks about; 'my brudder' this and 'my brudder' that." Blake chuckled. "I hope we can stick together this go around. Vari will kill me if we don't."

"We will." Alexus shifted her eyes to Blake's. "I've thought long and hard about this. There's no way I'm going to deprive myself of the love I want and deserve. Everybody wants me to be with T-Walk, but I'm going after what I want, and that's you."

"You still talk to that nigga?"

"No I haven't talked to him since that night at the club last year. We follow each other on Instagram and Twitter, but that's about it. I've been

38

avoiding MTN events just to stay away from him. His guys were the ones who kidnapped our son, you know. Plus, he's engaged to Thunder now, that girl from the reality show."

"Yeah, I heard about that."

"Yeah." Alexus sighed, looked down at the toes of her high-heeled white Chanel boots, and sighed again. "Never mind him, though. He's no longer a factor in my life. What has me worried is my crazy aunt, and the fact that the CIA sealed off our drug tunnel and cut ties with us after last year's bombings. They say we'll all be indicted if we're caught moving even a single kilo into the States. Of course, I'm worrying myself half to death over that, because the bombings in Mexico practically wiped out the Sinaloa and Zeta Cartels, so it's basically just me supplying coke to this country. I have ten submarines. Each one holds eight thousand kilos. We do two runs a month now; one coke, one green. Everything's running smoothly, but God only knows what'll happen if the feds ever catch wind of it."

Blake became thoughtful. He sipped a bit of lean while his other hand massaged the rear of the white leather pants Alexus had changed into after showering at the penthouse.

"Somebody bombed the Matamoros restaurant today. The media's all over it. And my cousin Antoney has gone missing." Alexus studied the gold and diamond money bag on his chain, then moved in a little closer and looked him in the eye. "I think my Aunt Jenny's involved. I think she's been lying low, planning and plotting, and now she's emerged from wherever she was hiding with an entirely new list of things to blow up, people to kill, and places to terrorize."

"I'm not surprised. Your whole family's crazy; the Mexican side, at least. That's probably why you're so damn crazy."

"You're the crazy one."

"Crazy about you," Blake smirked. "Look, I'm sorry to hear about that shit with your auntie, but I need in on them bricks. You know I can flip a thousand of 'em in a month; and once niggas see I'm getting' 'em like I used to, I'll triple that."

"I'll have whatever you want delivered to one of your friend's closest friend's closest friend, but nothing comes to you but the cash. The feds are following every person I associate with. I won't have you getting locked up for trafficking drugs. You're the richest guy on the black music scene. Let the guys with only twenty or thirty million in the bank be the drug bosses. You're the boss of all the bosses, and I'm…" Alexus hesitated.

"You're what?" Blake pecked his lips against the bridge of her nose. "I don't know. The queen of all queens, I guess. Or the cocaine

princess." She snickered once. "Gave myself that name the night you and T- Walk shot each other last—"

The thunderous boom of a gunshot stunned Alexus into silence.

Savaria wrapped her arms around King Neal, let out a frightened yelp, and looked to her father for safety.

"Oh, my God, what was that?" Alexus murmured.

Blake snatched a Glock out of his hoody pocket. "Vari, take your brother back there to the bathroom and lock the door." He and Alexus eyed the top of the staircase a few feet away. "Every time you bring these fuckin' Mexicans around, I hear gunshots."

The recording studio door opened and the men of Money Bagz Management emerged. They too were toting Glocks with thirty-round clips and laser beams.

Just then, Enrique came walking up the spiral staircase. He had a gold-plated Desert Eagle .50-caliber in his hand, and smoke was drifting out of its barrel.

"Alexus, our men have brought you a few visitors. Come and see," he said in a casual yet cold tone of voice.

Then he turned and headed back down the stairs.

## *Chapter 8*

The conference room was ominously quiet.

A new video of Jennifer Costilla had just surfaced online. It was being played on the large wall-mounted television that took up most of the rear wall. The FBI agents were watching it for the third time in a row, and most of them were still cringing and looking away as the beheadings began.

Special Agent Sneed was not cringing, nor was he turning away from the gruesome footage. He was taking in every detail, studying every movement, listening to every sound, and taking notes on the small notepad he always kept in his breast pocket.

The three victims were already identified. They were Antoney Costilla, Jenny's brother Flako's son; Emilio Guzman, one of Mexico's most wanted drug traffickers; and Jim Mallory, Republican mayor of Brownsville, Texas. They had all been kidnapped from Alexus Costilla's restaurant just seconds before a suicide bomber walked in and blew the posh establishment to smoldering pieces. Pacing back and forth in front of the dry-erase board, Director Byrd was paying close attention to the video. His eyes were stringent slits. His face was tight.

"Okay," he barked, "there are, what, ten thousand American troops in Mexico searching for this lady, am I right?"

"Fourteen thousand," Sneed corrected.

"Same difference. How'd she walk into that restaurant? And I thought we had tails on all the Costillas? Who was following Antoney?"

"Two of my men," said Special Agent Maxwell, a fifteen-year FBI veteran out of Houston. "They were both injured in the blast. Jenny was not present during the kidnappings, and her men were too heavily armed for those two agents alone. By the time they radioed for backup, the kidnappers were leaving and the suicide bomber was walking in."

Byrd shook his head. "She has to be somewhere in Mexico."

"What we need to focus on," Sneed said, "is this Matamoros Cartel.

I said it still existed, and Jennifer just confirmed it. I honestly believe this

drug cartel and the billions of dollars Alexus inherited are closely related. If I'm correct, this new video may be directed at Alexus and the rest of the Costilla family. It would explain why Jennifer chopped off her own nephew's head, and why Alexus' security detail is so sophisticated. It would also explain the numerous assassination attempts on Alexus over the past few years. There is no way to bug her phones, and her properties and vehicles are routinely swept for bugs, but we can get her. I say we start by questioning government officials in Brownsville, Texas. There's a reason Alexus' hometown mayor was in that restaurant. He may have been working with the Costillas, helping them move their product from one location to the next without being detected."

"Hmm." Director Byrd nodded. "Well, Sneed, since Alexus is in the Chicago area, feel free to take on this new investigation into her and this cartel. You have my approval, and if need be I'll give a shout to the DEA to assist you and your team in investigating the cartel. Just do me a favor, will you?"

"Anything, sir."

"Find out what Jennifer meant by 'the ten', and do it quickly."

## *Chapter 9*

There was a dead man lying in the foyer when Blake, his MBM crew, and Alexus made it to the first floor.

The guy's brains were splattered across the white marble floor. He was face-down, had a big hole just above his left ear, and his forehead was like an open window. He was an overweight Hispanic corpse in an expensive-looking gray suit.

A similarly dressed and shaped black man stood near the body with his hands raised in surrender. Four of Alexus' men had assault rifles trained on him, but he did not look afraid. Cautious maybe, alert, but definitely not afraid.

Alexus paused next to the brainless man, eyed him briefly, and said, "No more of this, Enrique. Not when my son is around."

"Nothing stops the family business," Enrique replied. "Besides, he deserved it. He walked in and said, 'Tell Alexus I'm not paying for that last shipment unless she lowers the price.' He never spoke to your father that way. Papi would have cut off his head."

The dead man was Frankie Sanchez, a forty-something, high-ranking Latin King out of upstate New York. Yesterday morning, a semi- trailer containing a thousand kilograms of pure Colombian cocaine had arrived at his sister's Patterson, New Jersey home. Knowing the kilos would be sold for at least $28,000 a piece, Alexus felt that her asking price of

$15,000-a-ki was more than generous.

Frankie had only paid half of the $15-million, and evidently that was all he'd been willing to pay.

Stepping over Frankie's fat body, Alexus grabbed her hips and looked his fat friend up and down. "Who's this guy?"

"I'm Jackson, from Harlem. Did some time with Frankie in the nineties. He was supposed to be introducing me to you guys. My Bloods out in Harlem are already getting big money, and we're paying thirty racks for every ki. Frankie owed me a favor. I asked to meet his connect."

Frowning, Alexus took a step back and turned to Enrique with a quizzical expression on her face. He read her perfectly.

"They're not wired," Enrique said.

43

"Good. Are my kilos still with this fat fuck's sister?" "Si."

"Okay, get them to this guy's people in Harlem," Alexus said, pointing at Jackson. "I want fifteen grand off each kilo, Jackson. A dollar short and your family dies. Comprende?"

Jackson nodded his meaty black head.

Shaking her head, Alexus walked back to Blake's side and, gazing at Frankie's gaping forehead, decided it was best to issue yet another order.

She said, "Gas up the jet, and send somebody to pick up my therapist. We're going to Mexico for a few days, and I need someone to talk to while I'm there."

The iPhone 5 on Alexus' hip started singing a Beyoncé tune. She answered it on the second ring. It was Tasia.

"Girl," Tasia said, "your aunt has just released a video of her cutting off your cousin Antoney's head. It's all over the news, but they're not showing the full video. You can see the whole thing on Liveleak. Yo, she's talking to you in that video, Lex. Said something about she wants 'the ten', whatever the hell that means."

## *Chapter 10*

"She's talking about the ten submarines," Alexus said to Blake as they walked up the second-floor hallway to the bathroom where their children were hiding. "She knows we're supplying coke to ninety-five percent of the US with these subs, making thirty-million a day. I'm guessing she wants the subs to sneak some materials into the states for another attack."

Blake said, "Thirty million a day?"

"Yes, Blake. Sixty thousand kilos at fifteen grand a piece amounts to nine hundred million dollars, am I right? That's thirty million a day with the subs coming in once a month."

"Damn. That's a lot of money. My whole net worth in one month." "The money isn't important. What's important is making sure Jenny

never gets her hands on those subs."

"And making sure your crazy ass bodyguards don't blow any-more brains out in my house. Keep that bullshit in Mexico."

"Sorry about that," Alexus said, crossing her arms and biting a thumbnail as they stopped outside the bathroom door. "They're cleaning it up. Let's not worry over small things like that. Some folks are meant to die. Sometimes it's for the best."

Blake squinted his eyes and regarded Alexus with a question-ing look. He'd never heard her speak so ruthlessly. Usually she was the kindest girl in the world, sensitive and sweet. Violence always made her squeamish.

Had her heart turned cold over the past twelve months? Blake wondered this as he knocked on the bathroom door.

"Vari, it's me," he said.

Savaria unlocked and opened the door, glanced from Blake to Alexus and back to Blake. She was holding her little brother's hand. "Was that a gun sound, Daddy? It sounded like a gun."

Her question went unanswered. Blake muttered, "Come on," as Alexus hoisted King Neal up onto her hip and they took the rear staircase down to the first-floor hallway where Blake's bedroom was located, perambulated through the spacious Highland Park mansion's lavishly furnished rooms, and finally exited into the massive garage. Kanye's black Maybach was gone. Alexus' bodyguards were present, and Enrique was standing beside the rear passenger door of Alexus' Rolls Royce limousine.

Alexus and the kids got in first and Blake and Enrique climbed in behind them. It was a 13-passenger limo, so there was plenty of room.

Enrique said, "That Jackson guy...?"

"Bury him with Frankie," Alexus replied instantly. "He could be a fed for all we know."

"Tasia and Cereniti are meeting us at the airport." "Then we can head out now."

"Sure thing." Enrique mumbled a few Spanish words into the thin mic that extended from his ear to the side of his mouth.

Blake was again giving Alexus the look. She turned to him and her brows knitted.

"What?" she asked, fluctuating her eyes from his to the macabre Jenny Costilla video she was watching on her smartphone.

"You're not the same Alexus I remember being with."

"Of course I'm not. I'm the boss of the world's number one drug cartel, CEO of a multibillion-dollar corporation, and above all else I'm a Costilla." She showed a forced smirk. "The old me is long gone, and the new me is figuring out a way to make Aunt Jenny pay for nailing my mom to that cross."

## *Chapter 11*
## **The Next Morning**

Trintino "T-Walk" Walkson was in the middle of an Ebony Magazine cover shoot in the front yard of his childhood home in Michigan City, Indiana when he got the call.

The city was blanketed in snow. It was early, a quarter after seven on a cool January morning, and hardly anyone was out. A couple of teens were eyeing the photo shoot from across the street; smoke from the exhausts of the four Escalades at the curb clouded their view.

After issuing an apology to the photography team, T-Walk dug in his powder blue Armani suit jacket for the vibrating mobile phone. He smiled affably at Tasia's contact picture. She'd been like a sister to him ever since she and Bookie, T-Walks childhood friend, had started dating a few years prior.

"What you want, Tay? I'm at a photo shoot for the cover of Ebony, so make it quick."

"A photo shoot? This damn early?"

"Yeah. It's a 'rags to riches' story, and you're interrupting it. Is this important?"

"Kinda." Tasia paused, sighed. "It's Alexus. She's, umm… fucking around with Blake again."

T-Walk gritted his teeth together and glowered at a mass of dirty snow next to the stone walkway of his parents' old clapboard home.

Hearing Blake's name never failed to infuriate him, and it wasn't just because Blake had shot him four times in the past, or the fact that Blake had gunned down more of his friends than he could count on both hands.

No, T-Walk's harsh feelings toward Blake began and ended with Alexus Costilla, the girl they both loved, the beautiful young billionaire who'd made the two of them financially strong and emotionally weak. Thanks to her, T-Walk was now one of the television industry's biggest

producers, with seven reality shows on three different networks, all of which were owned by Costilla Corp.

"We're all here at the mansion in Matamoros," Tasia continued. "You should see the security she had here, yo. Shit's mad crazy.

Everybody's afraid Jenny will somehow blow the place to the moon while we're here."

"Is that why you're calling me?"

"No, it's not. I'm calling to let you know that Blake will be in Miami tomorrow for a big video shoot with Diddy and Rick Ross, and afterwards he'll be at Magic City for his mixtape release party. I overheard him telling Alexus about it last night."

"And?"

"You know what I'm saying. Read between the lines. Yo, you are mad soft if you've forgiven him for shooting you. What about Squirm, and Lil Regg, and KG? Blake's running all over your team, yo, killing all your guys and rapping about it like he's Chief Keef's twin. Shit's got you lookin' mad weak in the streets. People saying you went Hollywood, like you ain't a G no more. Money don't mean nothing if niggas don't feel you when they see you. Don't fuck around and get your ghetto pass revoked. Send some niggas at this clown and get it over with."

T-Walk's scowl deepened. He gave a tight-faced head nod to a passing MCPD patrol car. Officer Lay, Drug Abuse Resistance Education teacher for the city's elementary schools, was behind the wheel. His bald black head returned the nod, and he kept it moving.

Little did Tasia know, it was Alexus who'd blown Squirm's brains out in the office at T-Walk's nightclub. But there was logic to Tasia's argument: Blake *had* killed Lil Regg, KG, Johnny, Lil Steve, and a few more of T-Walk's closest friends.

The photographers were becoming irritated. "I'll talk to you later," T-Walk said.

"Don't let the chance to get this nigga slide, yo," Tasia persisted."I'll take care of it," T-Walk said and hung up.

## *Chapter 12*

Alexus' mouth and eyes were agape, and short, orgasmic breaths were blowing from her parted lips, accompanied by whimpering moans every time Blake sank his glistening black phallus in her lubricious pussy. Her fingernails clawed his upper back as she succumbed to her fourth climax of the morning.

"Oh, my God, don't stop, don't stop. I'm cummiiiing," she said, panting and enjoying the feel of Blake's powerful chest against her undulating breasts.

They were in Alexus' master bedroom inside of her sprawling Matamoros mega-mansion. Her bed—large and round and blanketed in white fur—was covered in $10,000 bundles of bank-new hundred-dollar bills. Blake had dumped $2 million on the bed before their raucous episodes of passionate sex began; and now, a full three hours later, over half of the cash bundles were on the floor, victims of Blake's relentless thrusts and Alexus' occasional escape attempts.

Blake rose up, still holding her legs back and delivering the deep penetrations he knew she loved so much. Her legs were trembling in his hands. Tears were in the corners of her eyes.

"I can't take it anymore, Blake. It's too much. Stop. Please."

But he did not stop. Instead, he turned her over, lifted her to her knees, pushed the back of her head down until her face was buried I the pillow, and again sank his pole deep into her sopping goodies.

He held onto her hips and fucked her roughly. Alexus' loud moans filled the room. The sight of her wobbling derriere sent him over the edge a mere two minutes later. He yanked out of her and shot several ropes of semen onto her ass and down the middle of her back.

Forty-five minutes later, the two of them were showered and dressed for the warm Central American winter weather. Blake donned a black Nike t-shirt with matching gym shorts and sneakers, and Alexus wore a white Gucci halter over small denim shorts and sneakers by the same designer.

Walking out of the massive bedroom ahead of Blake with her eyes glued to her smartphone, Alexus was already in deep thought. She had over thirty million Twitter followers and close to fourteen million Instagram followers, and the majority of them were commenting on the Jenny Costilla video.

"This shit is getting outrageous," Alexus said aloud to herself.

"I know." Blake was keeping pace next to her, studying his own smartphone. "Snoop just retweeted a CNN article about it. 'Why Jennifer Costilla is more dangerous to the US than any terrorist in history.' Your auntie is just as nuts as Papi was."

Alexus cut an accusatory glance at Blake. "If your smart ass knew how to properly use a gun, Papi would be here to handle Aunt Jenny."

"I apologized for that."

"Yeah, but apologies won't bring my father back to life. You are so lucky my family doesn't know who shot him. Uncle Flako would be all over you in a heartbeat and you know it."

"I said I'm sorry."

"Let's not talk about this, okay? My morning has been great thus far and I intend to keep it this way."

Out of the corner of her eye, she saw Blake shrug his shoulders dismissively. Just seeing his dismissive gesture made Alexus' blood boil, and she had to remind herself that she loved him dearly. Otherwise, she'd have pulled the gold-plated .45 caliber pistol out of her big leather shoulder bag and blasted him in the chest.

A breakfast of sausages, buttery pancakes, grits, and cheese-drenched scrambled eggs awaited them in the dining room. Melonie, the therapist, and the girl who'd flown in with her—a pretty brown girl named Tamera—were already sitting at the long table with Tasia, eating and confabulating in hushed tones. Enrique and three other bodyguards were chatting before the fireplace.

"Somebody's glowing," Melonie commented, beaming at Alexus.

"I'm not glowing." Alexus cracked a smile as she took her seat at the head of the table. Blake sat to the right of her, directly across from Tasia. As her personal chef, a Virginian black woman named La'Tonya, place a steaming plate before her, Alexus said, "Sure hope my therapist isn't divulging any classified information over there."

"I'd never do that," Melonie assured.

Tasia eased forward in her chair and pointed a forkful of eggs toward Alexus. "I'll tell you what's not classified. You and Blake have been going at it for five hours, yo. Straight porn-star action. This is the biggest house I've ever in my life been in, and we've been hearing your moans and screams all damn morning. You need to get that bedroom door soundproofed or something. I'm glad the kids are out at the stables with Cereniti, or else King would've been crying and thinking you were getting murdered in there."

*'I was getting murdered,'* Alexus thought to herself. Her legs were still tingling, and her vaginal muscles were aching, but she wore the most illuminating smile. Blake had really put it on her.

"You know," Melonie said, "you're my wealthiest client by far, Alexus, but I don't do house calls. I'm gonna have to get going today."

Alexus shook her head. "I'm going through too much right now. I need someone to talk to about this stuff. I'll pay a grand and hour, and that's from the time we left Chicago until you make it back. Same for your friend. That okay?"

Tamera nodded excitedly; Melonie rolled her eyes, sighed audibly, and continued eating.

A minute or so later, Tasia's fork clattered down onto her empty plate. She wiped her mouth with a napkin and shifted her attention to Blake, who was devouring the palate-pleasing breakfast that sat before him while texting on his smartphone. Ogling his gaudy gold and diamond jewelry, she said, "I see you're still excelling in the music industry. Richest guy in hip- hop last year I heard, yo. Congratulations."

"Right on." He looked at her briefly, flashed a diamond-encrusted smile, and went back to texting.

"Is that all I get, yo? Just 'right on'? You feelin' some type of way about me or somethin'? 'Cause you can speak on it. Word up, yo. Where I'm from in Harlem, people don't bite their tongues. Let that shit out. You know I won't hesitate to speak my mind and say all the shit I don't like about *you*."

Pinching the bridge of her nose between her thumb and forefinger, Alexus sighed. "Don't, Tasia. Please."

"No," Tasia sailed on, "I'm not doing anything wrong. Blake,

51

you've broken my girl Lexi's heart too many times to count; you shot her cousin, Bookie, who was *my* boyfriend at the time; and word on the streets is that *you* are the one who killed Lexi's dad behind the club the night you and T-Walk shot each other. I have a ton of reasons why I shouldn't like your black ass."

Blake put his phone down and stared at Tasia for a long moment. His expression was indecipherable, but Alexus knew him well enough to know that he was angry and ready to snap.

Things never ended well when Blake was angry.

He was just about to lash out at Tasia when Enrique's head dipped in next to his.

"Senor," Enrique said, "your gifts have arrived. They're coming in

now."

Momentarily, Blake's anger diminished. He turned to Alexus and

studied her perfect, reddish-brown face as a long line of young women spilled into the room carrying bouquets of white roses, furry white teddy bears, and dozens of shopping bags from some of Houston's swankiest designer stores.

Alexus gasped happily, surprised.

"Blakey! Baby, you did this?" she muttered softly.

"Of course I did," Blake boasted as he stood up and picked a rose from one of the bouquets. "Ordered it all online this morning when I first woke up. Bought you a bunch of bags and shoes from some of your favorite

designers: Gucci, Louboutin, Louis Vuitton, Chanel, Prada— you name it, I bought it. The roses" – he helped her out of her chair and presented her the single rose – "symbolize a fresh, new beginning for me, you, and the kids."

Alexus twirled the rose beneath her nose, inhaling the wonderful scent of it. She locked eyes with Blake, and for a couple of eternal seconds the two of them gazed at each other and said nothing. They did not need to talk. Blake's affectionate surprise spoke volumes.

"Awww," Melonie cooed tearfully. "This has to be the sweetest thing I've ever witnessed."

"And that thousand dollars an hour," Tamera added, "is the

52

sweetest thing I've ever *heard*!"

Blake cracked up laughing; and Alexus, with tears in her eyes, did the same. Melonie and Tamera immediately joined in the laughter.

Tasia didn't find anything funny.

After peeking inside a few of the shopping bags, Alexus instructed a bodyguard to lead the gift-bearers to her bedroom and to have them leave the bags and bears and roses on her bed. Blake noticed she was happier as they sat back down to finish breakfast, and it warmed his heart to know that he was the source of her happiness. She was beaming. Her sweet green eyes were unwaveringly glued to his. She leaned toward him and poked out her lips for a kiss. Blake studied her succulent kissers for a second before pecking his lips against them.

"You two so belong together," Melonie commented, wiping tears from her eyes. "Sorry, I always get emotional when I see even the smallest gestures of love."

"Oh, please," Tasia cut in snidely. "He'll have her heart broken in fifteen pieces by the weekend."

Alexus sucked her teeth and rolled her eyes, two of the many idiosyncrasies she'd inherited from her mother. "Tasia, why can't you ever just be happy for me? Do you like seeing me single and lonely, texting you and Cereniti all day?"

Blake's anger instantly returned. He reached to the floor beside his chair and opened the extra-large Louis Vuitton duffle bag he's brought in from the bedroom. Inside it was the two million dollars I hundreds he and Alexus had defiled all morning, and the gold-plated .45-caliber pistol Alexus had given him when they arrived at the mansion last night. He liked it because the 50-round drum that was clipped to it was also gold-plated, as were the shells of the fifty hollow-tipped bullets inside the drum.

He took the drum out of the duffle and set it on the table with its barrel directed at Tasia. The mouths of Melonie and Tamera fell open; Alexus dropped and shook her head, eyes closed, pinching the bridge of her nose again.

But Tasia's cantankerous scowl remained.

"Lexi, you gon' sit here and let this nigga point a gun at me?" Tasia picked up her own iPhone5 and dialed a number.

Blake lifted the golden pistol, aimed it at Tasia's forehead, and through clenched teeth murmured, "Bitch, hang up that phone. If that's the police you're calling, I'm shooting as soon as you start talkin'. I already think you had a hand in my son's kidnapping the other year. Keep talkin' crazy."

"Nigga, fuck you and that gun. You ain't gon' do a damn thing wit' it," Tasia snapped as she stood and planted a hand on her hip.

Alexus said, "Sit down, Tasia. Hang up the phone. And please, will both of you *please* calm down?"

Shaking her head no, Tasia moved the phone to her mouth. "T-Walk, make sure y'all put at least a few more bullet holes in Blake's—"

BOOM!

The bullet punched a hole an inch above Tasia's left eyebrow and exited the back of her head with most of her brain in tow. She collapsed, flung rearward from the percussion, and tipped over her chair as she landed on the snow-white marble floor. The gold shell casing skittered across the table and became wedged in a pile of eggs on Melonie's plate.

"Blake!" Alexus exclaimed, rushing to Tasia's side.

Melonie and her friend pushed away from the table and attempted fleeing the room, but a wall of bodyguards halted them and Enrique instructed his men to hold the two women against the wall.

The smartphone Tasia had held was on the floor near her feet when Blake stepped around the table and picked it up. The call was still connected. He put it to his ear and listened:

"Tasia! Tay-Tay, you okay?" It was T-Walk's voice.

"Nah, nigga," Blake said, "this bitch ain't okay. Soon you'll be just like her. MBM gang, fuck nigga. Catch you in traffic I'm on one."

## *Chapter 13*

Rita Mae Bishop's crucifixion had made headlines worldwide, and the ensuing hunt for Jennifer Costilla made the story even more shocking to readers and viewers alike. She'd made a hasty recovery at the Victorian style mansion Alexus owned in The Hamptons, but the emotional and spiritual wounds remained; wounds that no amount of luxury or wealth could ever heal.

Now, sitting in the rear of her black on black Maybach with her eyes glued to her laptop computer, watching CNN's edited version of the Jennifer Costilla video while her driver cruised Lake Shore Drive, Rita felt those wounds opening again.

Tears sprang forth from her eyes and slid down her dark-hued cheeks.

Seated beside Rita was Britney Bostic, Costilla Corporation's number one attorney. She reached an equally dark hand over to Rita's laptop and slammed it shut.

"Stop looking at that evil woman. You'll ruin your makeup before we even make it to the restaurant," said Britney.

Rita cleared away the tears with the backs of her thumbs. "Sorry.

I'm just thinking of Flako and how devastated he must be. To have your son murdered in such a way, and by your own *sister*—I can only imagine how he's feeling right now."

"I agree with you one hundred percent. My condolences go out to him and his family. However, there is a fine black man waiting on you inside the Magnificent Mile's most popular restaurant, and I'm certain he'll be immediately turned off if you show up sad-faced and teary-eyed, especially on your first date."

The corner of Rita's mouth rose in a forced half-smile. With a sigh, she said, "Who is this fine black man you're speaking so highly of? Have I ever met him?"

"It's a blind date, Rita, a surprise."

"So what? You have to tell me who I'm eating lunch with. He could be married for all I know."

"He's not married. He's just as single as you are."

"Is he famous? Because you know I don't do too much mingling with those celebrities."

"He's not famous, either."

"For the love of God, Britney, tell me something. Did you play matchmaker? Did he contact you?"

"He emailed me last night and asked me to set up this lunch date. I knew you'd love it, so I set it up."

"Sure," Rita said, her tone replete with sarcasm, "can't you tell how unbelievably excited I am? Jumping for joy over here."

"Have you talked to Alexus?"

"Not since yesterday before her visit with the therapist. She sent me a 'good morning' video message earlier saying she was in Mexico—"

"In Matamoros?" Britney cut in.

Rita nodded. "I know that's not a particularly good place to be considering what happened with Jenny and the restaurant bombing. Alexus is probably there to comfort her Uncle Flako and his other two children. I'm sure there must be an army of men protecting that little town now. My daughter will be fine."

"I'd still check on her," Britney advised.

"Yeah, I suppose you're right," Rita said, digging in her Birkin bag for her smartphone. "I've got to tell her about this mystery date anyway."

## *Chapter 14*

"You're so fuckin' *stupid*!" Alexus screamed at the top of her lungs. "*Why*, Blake?! Why would you *do* something like this?! You didn't have to fucking shoot her!"

Blake gave no reply. Glaring down at Tasia's dead body, he showed not even a trace of remorse.

Cereniti had just pushed through the wall of bodyguards and was now standing next to Alexus with her hands covering her open mouth and her eyelids tremulous. They kept looking from Tasia to Blake. Melonie and her friend—calmer now but still badly shaken—were in the hallway just outside of the massive dining room with Savaria and King Neal.

"I knew it would come to this," Cereniti said in a near whisper. She wore a white mid-sleeved shirt over multicolored leggings and heels, and she was shaking all over. "When she told me she had set everything up for T-Walk and his crew to kidnap King Neal from that Chicago jewelry store, I knew either you or Blake would blow her head off. I just didn't think it would be so soon."

Alexus' expression changed. She went from staring angrily at Blake to gazing quizzically at Cereniti.

Blake said, "See, that's exactly what I said, ain't it?"

"You dirty bitch," Alexus said matter-of-factly. She crossed her arms and squinted at Cereniti. "So, you've known the entire time who was responsible for my son's kidnapping, and you're just now telling me this shit?"

"I couldn't say anything." Cereniti was now crying uncontrollably and rapidly shaking her head from left to right. "Me and Tasia have been tight since elementary school, yo. We were the baddest bitches in Harlem. When she told me about the kidnapping, I wanted to tell you, Lex. But I couldn't betray my bitch. I couldn't—"

BOOM! BOOM! BOOM!

Fire erupted from the barrel of Blake's golden pistol. The first round put a hole in the middle of Cereniti's chin, and the next two hit her high in the chest.

She was dead before she hit the ground.

## *Chapter 15*

Rita emerged from the plush confines of her sleek Maybach wearing a full-length black fur coat over a Prada pantsuit that was merely a few shades lighter than her deep brown skin. By the time Britney—clad in an equally extravagant fur—joined Rita on the sidewalk, they were already surrounded by armed guards in fresh black Gucci suits and matching trench coats. The men had swarmed out of the three black Escalades parked behind Rita's car before she'd even though of getting out.

"Is Alexus still not answering?" Britney asked as she breezed into the opulent Great Aunt Micki's restaurant ahead of Rita.

"I'll leave a voicemail for her to call—"

Rita's words trailed off into a stunned silence. Momentarily, she stopped breathing.

They were entering *The Red Room*, a back room where the wealthiest of Chicagoans often came to wine and dine, and beside the red- clothed table in the far right corner stood a man who Rita believed had been dead for several years.

It was her ex-lover, Neal Miller.

Tall, dark brown, and relatively handsome, he was dapper in a nice white button-up shirt with a vapid gray tie that matched his slacks and the sprinkles of gray in his hair.

Reluctantly, Rita continued toward him, feeling as if she were floating instead of walking, watching some strange Stephen King movie instead of observing reality. She heard Britney mutter something about messaging Enrique to check on Alexus, but Neal's warm smile held her spellbound. She wanted to fall into his outstretched arms, but she kept it sane and leaned in for a gentle embrace.

"You look amazing," he said in his gruff baritone.

"And you look alive." Rita took a step back and gave him a second head-to-toe examination. "Not too paralyzed, either."

"May I explain over lunch?"

"If the good Lord Jesus was not my savior I'd slap that smile right off your face. You've been alive this entire time, and you're just now revealing it to me?" She lowered her rump to the chair beside her, yanked her arms out of the sleeves of her coat, and pushed it down around her waist. "Get to explaining. I don't have all day."

Neal settled across from her, while Britney went to a nearby table with a dark-skinned young man Rita had never before seen.

There was a brief stare down between Neal and Rita. A few years prior, Jenny Costilla had detonated a C-4 explosive on Rita's front doorstep, leaving Rita with burns and a broken leg, and leaving Neal in a wheelchair, "supposedly" paralyzed from the waist down. Then, shortly thereafter, a hijacked plane was crashed into Alexus's Miami Beach home, and Neal had been presumably killed in the crash, though his body was never officially accounted for.

Now, Rita knew why he hadn't been found. The bastard was alive and well.

He put his elbows on the table, leaned forward, and said, "I apologize, Rita Mae. Sincerely. I was put in witness protection after that terrorist incident in Florida. The department forced me to stay away from you and Alexus. They moved me to New York and made me chief of the homicide division in Brooklyn. When I got fed up with the NYPD's bullshit twelve months in, you were already dating that MTN News guy, so I packed my bags and moved to Indianapolis. Invested all my savings in a sports

bar. Been doing pretty good so far."

Rita moved back in her chair and crossed her arms defensively. "Listen, Rita Mae," Neal went on. "I understand all this sounds crazy. But it's the truth, the whole truth, and nothing but the truth. That maniac Jenny Costilla had every police agency in the country on high alert. I was put in the witness protection program because my lieutenant at the Michigan City Police Department said I'd be endangering the city if I returned after being exposed to the Costilla family. Jenny was a terrorist then and she's an even bigger terrorist now. You've got to understand why I was forced to stay away."

"Hmm."

"What's that supposed to mean?"

"How are you walking all of a sudden? You were paralyzed last I checked," Rita said.

"I, uh—"

"You're full of it, Neal. I know it and you know it."

60

A slender black waitress was sauntering toward their table. Rita stood up, putting on her coat. She didn't believe a single word of Neal's explanation. She wished he would have just stayed wherever the heck he'd been, screwing whatever tramp he'd left her for.

"Will you please sit down and listen, Rita Mae? Please?" Neal pleaded.

"No, Neal. Go back to Indianapolis, okay. Leave me alone."

Neal attempted grabbing the sleeve of Rita's coat to stop her as she

turned to leave, but a perilously strong bodyguard pushed him back into his seat, and two more barrel-chested men moved forward to assist the pusher.

A wave of Rita's hand brought Brittney back to her side. Rita tried holding back the tears but they were burgeoning much too quickly.

"Don't you dare shed a tear, Rita. You know those damn paparazzi are probably already outside, and we are not giving them what they want.

Here, I have tissues in my bag. Wipe your eyes. And tell me why you're crying. I thought you'd be elated to see him."

They halted before reaching *The Red Room's* door. Rita accepted a Kleenex from her attorney and dabbed away the tears.

"He's lying to me, Brittney. God knows he is." "Lying about what?"

"He claims he's been in—" "Witness protection?"

"Yes," said Rita.

"He's not lying. I looked into it myself. He definitely worked a year with the NYPD. When he left there he opened a bar in Indianapolis, named it Man Cave I believe. Records show he's been there ever since.

Only thing he's lied about is the paralysis. My source at the NYPD says Neal was faking it the entire time in hopes of staying at your place long enough to get your daughter or Blake to reveal anything about those murders at T-Walk's club a few years ago. Two MCPD officers were killed in that shooting and Neal was in charge of investigating that case.

Everyone thinks Blake did it."

Rita let out a despondent sigh. It was a relief knowing that

Neal was forced to leave her, yet unsettling to know that he'd only stayed with her after the bombing to get Alexus and Blake to incriminate themselves in a multiple murder investigation.

She dug in her Birkin and retrieved a pair of Prada sunglasses.

Putting them on, she said, "No more blind dates."

A dozen men and women with shoulder-mounted video cameras and microphones were indeed out front as Brittney had predicted.

"Rita, what are your feelings on the suicide bombing at your daughter's restaurant in Mexico?"

"Rita, have you seen the Jenny Costilla video?"

The bodyguards made it easy for Rita and Britney to slide into the rear seats of the Maybach; and seconds later, they were being whisked away down Michigan Avenue.

## *Chapter 16*

The spacious office on the second floor of the Matamoros mega-mansion had once belonged to the late Vida Costilla, as had the entire estate. The décor was black, and just about everything— from the desk to the sofa across from it to the floor-to-ceiling bookshelves behind the desk— was trimmed in 24-karat gold.

Melonie Farr sat behind the desk, pale-faced, with a cognac laced cup of coffee on the desktop before her. She had her notepad in hand.

Alexus Costilla lay on the sofa, arms folded, knees up, tears cascading down into her ears, eyes focused on the gold chandelier that hung from the ceiling.

"I don't want you taking notes this session," Alexus said. "This day cannot be happening," muttered Melonie.

"I'm so sorry you had to see that Blake can be a real nutcase at times. He's been shot fourteen times altogether. I'd be a little crazy, too. Plus – wait, this is all confidential, right?"

"Absolutely."

Alexus inhaled deeply. "Ever heard of El Chapo?" "Can't say that I have."

"Well, he's the boss of the Sinaloa Cartel here in Mexico, a billionaire like myself, responsible for literally thousands of murders both here and in the U.S."

Melonie gave a nod, and Alexus continued.

"He's wanted by federal authorities here and in the states. They say he's the number one drug trafficker in all of Mexico." Alexus wiped the tears from her face; her unwavering gaze remained on the chandelier. "They're wrong. He's actually number two. There's another cartel boss who's been making around thirty million dollars every day; a supreme drug trafficker employing over three hundred thousand drug dealers and killers in Mexico and all over the U.S.; a drug cartel leader who's used to seeing what

just happened in my dining room. This cartel boss I speak of has enough legitimate cash to cover up the drug money. All of the Mexican politicians are on this person's payroll, as well as half of the United States' politicians. In fact, this person is the most powerful and wealthy drug cartel leader in history, like Pablo Escobar times three."

"Blake's a murderer, Alexus. None of what you're saying has anything to do with what he just did to those women."

"See," Alexus said, again wiping her face as she sat up and crossed her legs, "that is where you are wrong. I am the wealthiest, most powerful drug cartel boss in history. Blake was already a gangster when he and I met, and being around my cartel made him even wilder than he was before. I'm not happy about him killing those women, either. But they were snakes.

Friendly snakes. Cereniti stole five million dollars of my hard earned money not too long ago; and as we just heard, Tasia was behind my son's kidnapping. Who needs friends like those? I sure don't."

Melonie took a large gulp of her Hennessy and coffee mix, then sat the mug back down and gazed out the floor-to-ceiling windows to her left, shaking her head in disbelief.

"You're no drug cartel boss, Alexus." "You think I'm lying?"

"No not at all. I've heard of your father. You're just a young girl following in her father's footsteps, or at least trying to." Melonie turned to Alexus and sighed. "You don't need to be a drug cartel boss like your old man was. Your net worth is already $50 billion. You have more than enough money to live like a queen. Why involve yourself in the evils of the drug world? Even if you are this great drug lord living under the guise of a billionaire entertainment mogul, beneath it all you're still just an innocent young lady with too much money on your hands and not enough good people around you."

Alexus was shaking her head. "No, what I am is the daughter of a Mexican drug lord."

"And the daughter of a strong black Christian woman from Louisiana. Let's not forget that important little detail." Melonie stood up
from the soft leather swivel chair and carried her cup to the window.

Alexus joined her therapist at the window a few seconds later. They stood in silence, gazing out the window at the mile-long stretch of road that led up to the mansion. There was a solid white van driving down the road, and Alexus knew that the bodies of Tasia and Cereniti were inside it.

She cringed at the vision.

"You're right, Dr. Farr," she said finally. "I don't have the heart to run a drug cartel. But I've inherited the throne, and I have all the resources needed to keep it thriving and growing. Only thing missing is a cold-hearted decision maker, and maybe someone to keep me thinking clearly throughout all the drama. Blake can handle the decisions, and I'm pretty sure you'll stick around..."

"No Alexus."

"For ten million a year?" Melanie sighed again.

King Rio

## *Chapter 17*

Reclined in the sumptuous white leather passenger seat of Enrique's red Bentley Mulsanne, Blake "Bulletface" King was thumbing through a pile of hundred-dollar bills while eyeing the four white vehicles – a Bentley Continental GT and three Range Rovers – in his side-view mirror. The gun he'd used to kill Cereniti and Tasia was on his lap. They were traversing a winding back road near the Costilla mansion.

Enrique was following a white van.

"You're a lot like Papi, you know that?" Enrique's eyes never left the road. He detached his right hand from the steering wheel and showed Blake the tattoo on the back of it, two interlocking C's over a pile of cash, kilos of coke, and a golden machete. "Tell me what this means. You should know by now."

"I know what it means. Papi had it tatted on his chest, and Alexus got it on her left foot. Stands for Costilla Cartel."

Enrique gave a nod. "This tattoo has power behind it, like the sign of the Freemasons. Alexus has over $50 billion in legitimate cash and about

$70 billion in drug money. She's the queen of America, and she's chosen you to be her king. I pray that you never take it for granted." He turned and regarded Blake with a stern expression. "You've broken her heart several times already. You won't live to do it again."

The treat registered, and if not for the golden AK-47s on the laps of the two gelid-eyed cartel thugs in the back, Blake might have lifted his own weapon.

"You threatening me?" Blake asked in disbelief. "Don't let this rap start shit fool you. I was a gangsta nigga way before I was a CEO. That threat shit don't move me. I'm ready to die every day."

"Yeah?" Enrique let out a dry chuckle. "It just occurred to me why Papi had such a big problem with you dating Alexus. You're just like him, every bit as ruthless and opportunistic, cold and cunning. You may be a wild young black kid, but you're a wise one. You'll do well with the queen."

Blake couldn't help but to grin at Enrique's choice of words, for he knew that Alexus was indeed both the queen of America and the queen of Mexico's most lucrative drug cartel, while he himself was the king of the rap game. Together, he and Alexus were like Jay-Z and Beyoncé on steroids. The two of them would be unstoppable.

His attention moved to the road. The white van turned left and Blake's eyes widened at what blocked the road ahead.

There were four military tanks and a host of Mexican soldiers blocking a tall wrought-iron gate. Blake could see a massive warehouse behind the gate.

The tanks and soldiers moved to the sides of the dusty road. The gate screeched as it slid open.

Easing his luxury sedan into the warehouse parking lot, Enrique said, "Welcome to the land of cocaine."

## *Chapter 18*

In the car, Blake had been thinking of the scheduled video shoot in Miami and the $2 million he'd rake in for the Magic City show shortly afterwards. He had a row of ten Louis Vuitton suitcases sitting against the foyer wall at the Matamoros mansion, each filled with $7 million of the Costilla Cartel's hard-earned drug money, and he planned on blowing at least a million of it at the strip club.

But the entire idea of Miami dropped from his mind with the speed of lightening as he and Enrique breezed past a duo of armed soldiers and into the four-story warehouse.

Hundreds upon hundreds of white bricks were stacked together in bales that nearly reached the ceiling on both sides of the massive, steel- walled warehouse. What seemed to be a thousand naked Mexican women bustled around long steel tables that were covered in piles of what Blake logically guessed was cocaine. Several forklifts were loading bales onto semi-trailers at seven loading docks in back.

"You bullshittin' me," Blake uttered incredulously.

"Yes," Enrique said, smiling for once, "this is the land of cocaine, the place where your queen's workers weigh and package the majority of the kilos your country's drug-dealers break down and sell every hour of the day. Believe it or not, it's been here for years. All the presidents, vice presidents, mayors, governors, police, federal agents, and especially the bankers – they know of this operation, and they say nothing. They accept their payments and turn a blind eye to the blood that stains their wealth.

Corruption lies at the root of the drug trade; we cartels are merely the face of it."

Blake was too shocked to reply. Never in his wildest dreams could he have envisioned so many bricks of cocaine. There were thousands of kilos stacked almost to the ceiling. M-16-toting Mexican soldiers in black face-masks and camouflage uniforms were pacing up and down the aisles, standing near the tables and beside the loading docks.

They stopped in the middle of the warehouse. Blake flicked his eyes around at the nude women, most of whom were as young,

69

pretty, and steatopygic as Alexus Costilla.

Enrique said, "I've dealt with a few of your rapper friends—Jeezle, Rick Ross, that Gotti guy from Memphis, Birdman, Big Meech, Game Meek Mill, Fab, Juelz Santana, French Montana, that Gucci fella—the list goes on and on. But none of them have ever visited this warehouse. In fact, you're the first black guy who's seen this place. You should be honored."

"It's Jeezy, not Jeezle," Blake said with a short chuckle. He turned to Enrique, displaying his diamond grin. "I want ten thousand bricks delivered to my people in Chicago. I guarantee that all of 'em will be sold within two or three months."

"Your wish is my command," said Enrique.

## *Chapter 19*

Rita Mae Bishop had just sunk into her daughter's plush white leather sofa at the Trump penthouse when her smartphone began singing a Patti Labelle song. It was the ring tone she'd assigned to Alexus.

"That's her, isn't it?" Britney asked. She was seated next to Rita, sipping from a crystal stem glass full of red wine and checking messages on her iPhone 5. They'd stopped for lunch at Georgia Bees, another of their favorite soul food joints, and were now relaxing with their wine in hand.

The opening credits to *12 Years a Slave* were playing on the 100-inch Sony flatscreen across from them.

Rita pulled the phone from her bag and went straight to FaceTime. She instantly noticed the thinly-veiled pain in her daughter's expression.

"I got your voicemail," Alexus said. "It's been a crazy day in Matamoros, and the day's just begun. Ended up leaving my phone on the dining room table. Wasn't ignoring your calls."

"What's the down look about?"

"Nothing, mom. I'm fine. Never mind me; I wanna know about the date you mentioned in that voicemail. Brittany inboxed me on Facebook saying Neal was your date. Is she talking about Neal Miller? Is he alive?"

"Oh, he's alive all right, and he's not even paralyzed. I could have choked him, Alexus. God as my witness, I really could have strangled him at that table. Apparently, he was put in some sort of witness protection program after the plane attack in Miami. He went to New York for a while, now he's staying in Indianapolis."

"And you wanted to choke him for that? You should be happy he's alive and well."

"That's what I said," Britney chimed in.

Rita shook her head in disagreement. "He should have called. It's the least he could've done."

"Jesus, mama, don't you have a heart? I mean, I'm just as sur-prised about this as you are, but who can blame him for hiding out from the most dangerous terrorist in history. I'm about to go into hiding myself. Have you seen that video?"

"Yes, I saw it."

71

"She'd beheaded her own nephew, mama."

"That really shouldn't surprise you, Alexus. She's behind the bombing that killed a US president. And let's not forget she nailed me to a cross. Jenny Costilla is the devil. We'll never be safe as long as that evil woman lives. Honestly, I don't even feel comfortable with you being in Mexico after seeing that video. Especially since those men were kidnapped from your restaurant."

"Yeah... I know." Alexus paused. "I'll be fine. I've been waiting on Cereniti and Tasia to get back from their little shopping trip to Mexico City, but I'm leaving with or without them if they're not here when Enrique returns with Blake. We're flying to Miami and staying at the Versace mansion until after Blake's video shoot." A sneaky smirk crept across Alexus' perfect face. "Oh, did I mention that Blake and I are back together?"

The news was so disheartening that Rita ended the call abruptly. She turned to Britney and scowled.

"What?" Britney asked.

"You know what. Blake is not the man for my daughter. Have they been seeing each other behind my back?"

"Not that I know of. If they have, no one's made me aware of it." Britney was already dialing Alexus's number.

Alexus answered with a giggle. "Love you, ma!" she shouted loud enough Rita to hear. Then she was on speakerphone, and her every word was clear and precise.

"Listen, Britney: Blake's doing a show at Magic City tomorrow night, and I want every millionaire in hip-hop at that event. Call everyone.

Get my banker on the phone; I want five million in singles loaded into a Brink's truck and waiting somewhere near the club. Get Kay Slay on the phone and wire him a hundred grand to bring out the baddest models he's ever had in his magazine. Call Monica, Birdman, TI, Mary J, Future.

Contact all the hip-hop bloggers and magazines and let them know to start preparing the headlining articles, because the pictures they are about to receive will put all other Magic City nights to shame. I want animals – lions and tigers; I want the finest dancers in the South twerking on those poles; and lastly, I want breakfast with my mom and Neal at the Versace mansion first thing tomorrow morning."

Rita scoffed and rolled her eyes. "Excuse me, Alexus Costilla, but do I need to remind you who's the parent and who's the child in this situation?"

She waited on a reply, but Alexus had already ended the call.

King Rio

## *Chapter 20*

Blake didn't know who was in the white Bentley coupe that had trailed Enrique's car to the cocaine warehouse until they returned to the mansion. He was glad he had his golden .45 in hand when he finally saw its driver.

Short and a bit overweight with slightly graying hair and bloodshot eyes, Flako Costilla stepped out gripping his own gold-plated pistol. He started to raise the gun, but Blake was already aiming at is forehead.

"You!" Flako sneered. "You were there the night Papi was killed!

Which one of you murdered my brother?"

"Man, if you up that strap I'ma blast yo bitch ass. Enrique, you better get this muhfucka 'fore I start shootin'. You know I will." Blake's finger was tensely on the trigger. He'd already been shot fourteen times before; letting it happen again was out of the question.

Lucky for Flako, his equally chunky daughter, Bella, barged out of the white Bentley's passenger door and waddled around to her father's side. Though Bella hated Alexus, she liked Blake a lot, and he felt the same way about her. She was a cute little fat girl, half black like Alexus, always dressed in the finest of dresses and heels. She snatched the gun from her father's hand and tucked it inside her peach-colored Chanel bag, which matched her stunning dress and Louboutin heels. Bella was one of the select few who could calm Flako's volcanic temper.

"Settle down, father. He's a part of the family. Blake would never have shot Papi." Bella flicked a glance at Blake. "Right?"

"You think I'd be here if I shot Papi?" Blake asked. Animosity painted his dark face. Reluctantly, he lowered the gun. "I completely understand your anger right now. Your own sister just killed your son and showed it to half the world. I'd be mad, too. But don't try to take it out on me."

Flako jabbed an accusatory index finger in Blake's direction, removed the cigar from the corner of his mouth, and issued an ice cold

threat.

"If I ever find out that it was you who killed my brother, you're dead, Blake. You listening? Your family will die, and then you will die. Comprende?"

## *Chapter 21*

Blake kept a wary eye on Flako as they walked into the mansion.

His smartphone was ringing and vibrating incessantly on his hip, but he was not about to slip up and take his attention off Alexus' perilous uncle.

They found Alexus sandwiched between the kids on the living room sofa, their eyes on the animated movie on the wall-mounted television across from them, their hands buried wrist deep in the large bowl of popcorn on Alexus's lap. Dr. Melonie Farr was drinking coffee in an easy chair in the far corner, and like a loyal pet, her friend Tamera was standing next to the chair.

Alexus handed the popcorn over to Savaria, and then stood as Flako walked to her. She hugged him tightly, a long hug, and suddenly the old guy was crying. Bawling. His heavy body bounced beneath his expensive white suit as he sobbed in his niece's arms. Bella added her arms to the hug, as well as her tears.

Enrique whispered into Blake's ear, "Sad day for the Costilla Cartel, you know. Antoney was a good guy. Never hurt anybody, took good care of his wife and keys and kept them away from the business. He's the fifth Costilla to be killed in the past three or four years. Sad. I hate to see it.

Pedro's probably somewhere drinking himself to death now. Can't imagine how it must feel to lose a brother in such a brutal way."

"That crazy bitch, Jenny," Blake shook his head.

"Yes. She is indeed one crazed woman. But then again, what drug cartel member isn't a little off? All these murderers would turn even the warmest hearts cold. Alexus will be just as murderous soon enough. I'll bet my life on that."

## *Chapter 22*

Alexus Costilla was one of the few celebrities with a private landing strip behind her home. The Gulfstream 650 she'd squandered $70 million on a year prior was gassed up and ready for takeoff when she, Blake, the kids, and her entourage boarded the private jet. Its interior reminded Blake of a hallway full of thick, white leather chairs.

He settled across from Alexus, and his daughter sat on his lap while Enrique laid the sleeping King Neal in the reclined chair across the aisle from Blake.

Minutes later, they were in the air.

"Told my mom about us getting back together," Alexus said, opening a laptop computer on the table in front of her. "She flipped. Hung up on me. I knew she'd be mad, but not *that* mad. She's never hung up on me before."

"She'll be a'ight. I'll talk to her," Blake replied confidently, smiling his diamond smile and administering a comforting rub to his daughter's arm as she rested her head on his shoulder.

"Daddy, did somethin' happen to the girl who took me and my brother to ride the horses this morning? 'Cause when I was outside the eating room today, I heard a gun. My brother heard it, too."

Blake planted a kiss on Savaria's forehead. "We'll discuss this later, okay? When we get to Miami. Here," he gave her his iPhone. "Go sit over there by your brother and call your grandma. Let me talk to Alexus for a minute."

He sat back and gazed at the beautiful woman across from him. She'd changed into a small white t-shirt over skin-tight leggings and six inch heels of the same color. Without looking up from her computer she said, "Aunt Jenny really put the heat on me when she mentioned the Matamoros Cartel in that video. I'm wondering how she even knew enough about my operation to demand I give her the exact number of subs I'm currently using. Someone close to me had to have given her that information. I know it couldn't have been Enrique."

"She probably got Antoney to tell her everything before she made that video," Blake surmised.

"Yeah... I guess so. But who knows." She shut the laptop and looked at Blake. "Guess what? I just terminated T-Walk's contract with Costilla Corp., and legally there's nothing he can do about it. The reality shows he created belong to my corporation, and there's nothing he can do about that, either. From now on, he's permanently barred from attending any and all events associated with Costilla Corp. and all our sub-companies. He'll never make another dime if I have anything to do with it. I'm sure Time Warner or News Corp. will pick him up. I don't care, as long as he's not with me. That bastard had my son kidnapped. He's lucky if I don't have him killed."

"You ain't even gotta worry about that, baby. He won't be around for too much longer. I'm waitin' on him to touch down in Chicago again. Got some hittas out there that's gon' make sure he dies this time. I swear, in the back of my mind, I knew he was involved in King's kidnapping, just like I know that it was him who had mu Bugatti shot up in Chicago the night all that shit went down last year. Couldn't prove it, but I definitely knew it." Blake cracked a smile. "Speaking of Chicago, why did you shoot Cup like that? Luckily, he had a bulletproof vest on that night."

"Screw Cup. He got us out of a fifty- million-dollar ransom. I should have shot him in the face."

"Yeah, but we've made a few hundred million off him and his gang since then. Trust me; I don't like that nigga at all. He had my daughter's mother killed. I'll never forget that shit. But your pops taught me to never mix feelings with business. With that being said, it's best to keep him alive and well as long as he's making us money. Feel me?"

"Not really," said Alexus.

"What did Flako and Bella want?"

"Permission to send some men to Venezuela. Flako thinks Aunt Jenny has been hiding out there. I'm sending four hundred men, real official-looking military guys in helicopters and Humvees. Hopefully, we'll learn something. If I can get Jenny out of the picture soon enough, no one

will care to investigate the Matamoros area for an alleged drug cartel. The US will claim victory, and all will be good.

Alexus stood, and Blake's eyes went to her hips... her meaty thighs... and the clear vaginal print between them. She was obviously naked beneath the leggings, and seeing it made Blake's

80

mouth water.

He got up, grabbed her hand, and sprinted up the aisle to the restroom. She stumbled along behind him, giggling merrily.

"Boy, what the hell is wrong with you?" Alexus asked as he pulled her into the restroom and kicked the door shut.

"You know what's wrong with me." Blake lifted her onto the sink and mashed his lips against hers. "Think you gon' wear some tight ass pants with no panties in front of me?"

"You're a freak, you know that?" "Yup."

He started sucking and kissing her lips again, and she did the same to him. He lifted her shirt over her head and then snatched off his own white tee, exposing the sharply defined muscles that bulged from every inch of his upper body. His dick made a tent in the crotch of his True Religion jeans, which were also white like the Louis Vuitton belt on his waist and the matching sneakers on his feet.

"Lock the door," Alexus murmured, peeling off her leggings. Blake engaged the lock with a flick of his wrist and was back to

Alexus half a second later. She was now down to her white-lace bra and Louboutin heels. Her pussy was smoothly shaven, and Blake wasted no time in lifting and parting her legs for a taste.

He flickered his tongue on her clitoris, gripping and squeezing her outer thighs in his strong black hands. The delicious scent and taste of her pussy made him never want to stop licking and sucking. There was only one fifty-billion-dollar pussy in the world, and knowing this compelled him to suck even harder.

He was only four or five minutes into this episode of cunnilingus when Alexus began moaning and gyrating her hips ecstatically. A tremulous orgasm ensued. Blake took a few steps back and unbuckled his belt, silently admiring the juices that were squirting out of her. She dropped her head back and moaned repetitively, massaging her clit in small circles with her impeccably manicured fingertips.

Blake thought, *'This is Alexus Costilla I'm looking at, the baddest reddish-brown skinned, curvaceous-bodied young woman since Beyoncé; the CEO of one of America's most lucrative and financially superior corporations; the queen of the wealthiest, most powerful drug cartel in history. And she's all mine.'*

He could not repress the surfacing smile as he pushed his jeans and boxers down to his knees and moved forward until the head of his foot-long phallus was touching Alexus' wet, pulsating vaginal opening.

"You are the baddest bitch ever, baby. No disrespect meant." Blake kissed her lips once, twice.

"None taken, Alexus said, returning his kiss. "I had to be the baddest bitch to gain the attention of Bulletface, am I right? Mr. King of the Midwest." She grinned widely, then gasped as he penetrated her with over half of his rigid pole.

Alexus dug her fingers into his powerful back, holding her breath at his every inward thrust and exhaling heavily at his every outward thrust.

Blake sucked on the left side of her neck, just an inch or so below her ear, because he remembered that it was the one spot on her body that never failed to send her into fits of ear-pleasing moans.

This time was no different.

## *Chapter 23*

When Britney got up in the middle of their movie and left the living room, Rita never expected her to return a few minutes later with Neal Miller and the handsome young man Britney had sat with at the restaurant.

"You've got to be kidding me," Rita said.

"Not at all," Britney smile cheerfully. "I believe you two have some making up to do. Patrick and I will be back shortly. You all play nice." She took hold of the handsome man's hand, and together they exited the condo.

Rita got to her feet, crossed her arms over her chest, and waited on Neal to speak.

"My goodness," he said, crossing the room to gaze out of one of the tall glass windows. "You must have paid a *fortune* for this place. How high up is this?" When Rita didn't reply, he turned to her and copied her cantankerous stance. "You're not going to let me off easy, I see."

"Why should I?"

"I don't know. Because I love you. Because I've never lied to you or mistreated you. Because I was with you before all the glitz and glamour of the life you're now living."

"So, you've never lied to me, Neal? Ever?"

"One time, Rita Mae. When I was in the wheelchair, I was taking shots to keep my legs numb so my cover wouldn't be blown. Blake was suspected of killing two of my officers, and as chief homicide detective, it was my job to build the case against him. Aside from that one instance, I've never lied to Rita Mae Bishop. I can swear to that on a stack of bibles."

"Hmmm." Rita put her hands on her hips.

"I'm serious, Rita Mae. I'd never do anything to hurt you, and you know it. You can even ask Patrick. I've been telling him about you ever since the day he walked into my sports bar."

"Who is he?"

"Just some kid I met. He's from Forty-second and Post Road, a neighborhood in Indianapolis where almost everyone sells drugs. Met him the night his brother was shot and killed in Haughville, a rival neighborhood on the west side of town. Patrick came into the bar and ordered a drink. He told me what had just happened to his brother; said he'd had enough of the drug game, that he wanted to straighten up and fly right. I gave him an open waiter position at the bar, and now he's an assistant manager. Not the best pay, but it keeps him out of the streets, you know?"

Shaking her head, Rita refilled her wine glass and downed half of it in a single gulp. Deep down she knew that she was only rejecting Neal because she cared enough about him to keep him out of harm's way. Her last two lovers, Nat Turner and Fredrick Douglass, had both been brutally murdered by the Costilla family, and she didn't want Neal to end up like them.

He looked at the television and chuckled once. "Old habits truly do die hard. You're still obsessed with Denzel, I see. What's the name of this one? Think I may have seen it before."

"You're a real piece of work, Neal. You know that?" Rita felt and heard her voice cracking. "Do you think that I'm going to forget the fact that you abandoned me when I needed you most? Am I supposed to *forget* that? Huh, Neal? Am I supposed to just fall back in love with the man who's had me thinking he was *dead* for the past several years?"

The tears were already threatening to burst free as Neal walked over to Rita, and when he lifted her chin with the side of his index finger and gave her a soft kiss on the lips, they did just that.

## *Chapter 24*

*'MBM Gang in the buildin', bitch we kicked the doors in*
*I'm right back on the Dub nigga, soon's the fuckin' tour ends*
*Bulletface, Vice Lord, been goon since I was sworn in*
    *Shit you can ask the gangstas in the state that I was born in*
    *About me they'll tell you that I'm known to bring the Glock*
*'round Filled up wit' 30 hot rounds, disrespect me you get shot*
*down That's just how I was raised, how da gutta niggas got down*
*Shootin' you in ya braids'll make yo' mob niggas back down*
    *Put Dub Life hoodies on, and bring a hun'ed shots out*
    *The industry won't say you got wet up, they'll say you got*
*drowned...'*

"Maaan, why I the fuck are we listening to Bulletface? Ain't we supposed to be here to kill that nigga?" Bookie asked from the passenger seat of Craig's blood-red BMW 745.

"The nigga can rap. If I wanna listen to his music, I'ma do that.

Don't forget you in my shit, nigga. You can get the fuck out whenever you feel like it," Craig retorted, flipping open his Zippo lighter and lighting a Newport.

They were posted in the North Dolphin parking section at Miami International Airport, parked twelve spaces down from Blake King's matte black Bugatti Veyron Super Sport. It had pulled in ahead of the two black Escalades that were now parked on either side of it.

"What we gon' do," Bookie asked. "You see all these cameras, nigga? We can't shoot the nigga in here. Gon' have to catch him leavin', ride up on the side of that Bugatti at a red light or somethin' and let his ass have it."

"Gotta make sure Alexus ain't wit' him before we make any moves.

If I shoot your cousin, I'll have to shoot you."

Craig laughed but he was serious. He was a veteran drug dealer from the south side of Chicago, a slender, light-skinned man with diamond and platinum on his teeth and a glare of street wisdom in his eyes. He and Bookie were close friends, had been for years, and Craig knew that Alexus

Costilla was Bookie's cousin. Alexus was the sole reason why he and Bookie were living in million-dollar Miami homes, driving around Dade County in pricey foreign cars and SUVs, and discreetly selling hundreds of kilograms of the purest cocaine in the south. T-Walk has told them about the calls he'd received from Tasia the past two mornings, and they'd jumped at the chance to finish Blake off once and for all. In the past, Blake had shot Craig in the wrist, put a bullet in Bookies ankle, put *four* bullets in their dear friend T-Walk, and gunned down several more of their friends.

Bottom line, they wanted Blake dead.

And T-Walk was paying $10 million for the hit.

## *Chapter 25*

Cameras began flashing as soon as Blake and Alexus entered Miami International Airport. A flock of paparazzi appeared out of thin air. Alexus sat King Neal on her hip, Blake took Savaria's hand and, surrounded by luggage-wheeling bodyguards, they walked through the airport with their heads held high. Dozens of smartphone-savvy travelers aimed their camera lenses in Alexus and Blake's direction.

"This is exactly why I hate being famous," Blake muttered, glancing at the paparazzi. "These muhfuckas live to invade people's privacy. Let 'em hop out on me in the wrong situation. Bet they regret it."

"Don't let them get to you," Alexus said. "I'm not. Shit's just irritating."

"Well, don't let it irritate you. Are you riding with me to the Versace mansion? Enrique's already got my Mercedes van and a few SUVs waiting out front. You can just have the MBM crew meet us there, if you want."

"They're already here. They'll just follow us, and everybody else should be at the mansion by the time we get there."

"Everybody else?" Alexus asked.

"Yeah. I got a couple friends coming over." "*Male* friends, right?"

"Of course." Blake grinned. "You're the only woman I want in my life. You know that."

"Yeah right, Blake. You've been doing pretty good without me for a whole year, so you can miss me with that BS."

Blake chuckled heartily. He was feeling like a billion bucks. The short nap he'd taken on the 16-passenger jet after their restroom sex had him energized and ready to turn up.

"By the way," Alexus added snappily, "I hope you don't think we're about to be partying around the kids. You so-called *friends* better not be
expecting to act a fool with us today. I paid almost a hundred and thirty million dollars for that mansion, and I am not going to let your ratchet-ass friends tear it—"

"Grandmaaaaa!" Savaria screamed, cutting off Alexus' rant. She ripped away from Blake and ran to his parents, Dale and

Carolyn King, who were standing at the front of the airport with the Money Bagz Management recording artists.

King Neal wriggled his way out of Alexus' arms and ran behind his big sister.

Blake smiled at Alexus and said, "Let the kids chill with their grandparents while we're here in Miami. Momma wanna take 'em to the theme parks in Orlando anyway, and that'll give us some time to spend together."

"You thought this all out, didn't you?" Alexus accused. "Don't I always?" Blake took her hand in his and gave it an

affectionate squeeze. "I had Young-D bring out the Bugatti Super Sport. Wanna ride in that?"

## *Chapter 26*

Craig noticed that there was only one Escalade with the Bugatti when he caught up with it on Dolphin Expressway. He'd lost sight of the Bugatti twice since leaving the airport, which wasn't surprising considering it was the world's fastest production car.

Bookie was looking nervous in the passenger seat. His seat was reclined; he had cocaine crumbs stuck to the insides of his nostrils; beads of perspiration were stretched across his dark forehead; and he was holding his Mac-11 submachine gun so tightly in both hands that Craig thought it might break.

"We close to dat nigga yet, bruh?" Bookie asked.

"I'm a few cars behind. Just chill, bruh. Soon's they try to get off this highway, I'm pullin' up next to 'em. Make sure you hang out that window, 'cause I'm shootin' outta mine. And relax a lil bit, nigga. You act like the feds behind us or somethin'."

"You sure he in there?"

"Yeah, I'm sure. Told you I saw him in the driver seat." "And Alexus ain't wit' him?"

"Nope. I'm telling you, we got him this time. Just gotta make sure he don't live through it."

Craig was lying through his teeth. He hadn't spotted Blake in the Bugatti; the rear and side windows were too darkly tinted to see inside the multimillion dollar car. The thing was, Craig didn't give a fuck if Alexus was or wasn't in the car with Blake. The way Craig saw it, Alexus was holding out. She was worth $50 billion, yet she was only giving Bookie a hundred bricks of coke at a time, charging $15,000 for each kilo. She was being greedy, Craig thought, and he didn't care if she died with Blake. In fact, he hoped for it to go down that way.

"This shit gon' go down in history, bruh," Bookie said, sniffling and wiping his nose with the back of his hand. We about to take this nigga out the game like they did Pac in Vegas."

"Hell yeah," Craig murmured as the Bugatti turned onto an off-ramp. "Let's make history."

He pulled up along the Bugatti's passenger side and raised the Tec-9 from his lap.

The deafening sound of fully automatic gunfire filled the air.

King Rio

## Chapter 27

Blake was sitting in the back of the Mercedes Van with Alexus, Melonie, and Tamera when he received the tearful call from Mocha, his R&B artist.

"They just shot up Meach and Young-D! Some niggas in a red car just pulled up and started shooting!"

"What?!"

"We were on the off-ramp! I was right behind them! They're dead, Blake! Young-D and Meach are dead!"

Instinctively, Blake looked out the million-dollar van's side windows, as if he would be able to see his bullet-riddled Bugatti Veyron. The big white Mercedes Sprinter was soaring down MacArthur Causeway, just entering Miami Beach where the Versace mansion stood in all its glory.

"Are you okay?" Alexus asked, obviously noticing the pain in Blake's eyes. She'd been chatting with Melonie and Tamera about a Chanel gown they were looking at on their iPhones; now, however, Blake had her full attention.

He hardly heard the question. He hung up on Mocha, dialed his mother's number, and repeated Alexus' question.

"Yes, Blake. We're all fine. Jesus, we just left you at the airport. You can't trust me with the kids for thirty minutes without calling to check on us? Sit your butt down and focus on Alexus. You're always complaining and whining over how much you miss that girl; and now that you got her, you wanna call and bug me. Leave me and my grandbabies alone. Spend some time with your woman. Lord knows you need her."

And with that, Carolyn King ended the call.

Blake fell back in his sumptuous leather seat, dropping the iPhone to his lap and pressing the palms of his hands to his face. *'Not Meach and Young-D,'* he thought with an aching heart. *'Not my lil niggas.'*

"What's going on, Blake?" Alexus asked, worriedly.

"Somebody just... they shot up the Bugatti. Some niggas in a red car. Mocha say they killed Meach... and Young-D." He shook his head with his face still hidden in his hands.

"Oh, my God," Tamera murmured. "Meach is my favorite rapper.

Young Meach da Future; he's all I watch on YouTube."

"We know who's behind this shooting," Alexus said, "and you know how we're going to handle it. Enrique will have his head by sundown."

## Chapter 28

*Rapper Bulletface's Bugatti riddled with bullets on Miami highway...*

Seeing the words roll across the bottom of CNN brought a smile to T-Walk's mulatto face, and seeing his dick slide in and out of Ashley's mouth made him smile even harder.

He was lying in bed in his penthouse apartment at Miami Beach's Fontainebleau Hotel, basking in the oceanfront suite's midday sunshine while watching his 42" flatscreen television and enjoying his urban model fiancée's warm sucking mouth.

He looked up at the framed painting of Larry Hoover—legendary founder and leader of the Gangster Disciple Nation—that hung over the headboard of his king-size bed. He thought of the $42 million he had in his bank account, and of the dozens of bullets he was certain his goons had just served to Blake.

"I'm the *king* of this game, baby. On Larry Bernard Hoover, ain't *no*

nigga fuckin' wit' me. I'm too smart for these niggas; you hear me, baby? He thought I was gon' let him get away wit' that shit he pulled last year, like I'm dumb enough to let him live after he shot me *again*. Fuck I look like, *him*? This ain't that. Nigga must've thought this Hollywood shit turned me soft, baby. Had to be what he was thinkin'. Now the fuck nigga ain't thinkin' at all. He'll never think again."

The flawless chocolate model Ashley "Thunder" Hunter popped his dick out of her mouth and, licking its underside with the flat of her tongue, said, "Fuck that nigga, daddy. Fuck him and that Mexican bitch, Alexus. I hope they got her ass, too."

"Nah, Bookie wouldn't do that. That's his cousin."

"So what? It's not like she's doing anything for him. If I had a billionaire for a cousin, the bitch would at least have to give me fifteen or twenty million for myself, or I'd stop claiming the bitch."

T-Walk laughed heartily, and Ashley pursed her lips around the crown of his erection and continued sucking him. With her back arched the

way it was, T-Walk had a nice view of her thick rump, which

93

was as fat and round as Alexus Costilla's.

He closed his eyes and imagined that it was Alexus sucking him instead of Ashley. He remembered how Alexus used to swallow his semen and keep sucking when she gave him head; how she would deep throat him until she gagged. They'd fucked and sucked and licked and kissed each other in just about every place they'd visited, from their homes to their cars, to the swankiest hotel suites the world had to offer.

'Damn, I miss that girl,' T-Walk thought, opening his eyes and tensing as he spewed a thick load of semen into Ashley's mouth.

## *Chapter 29*

*'My Boys in the Hood keep the Mac Baby Boy if you wanna stunt Killa Season, The Goonies Unleashed, now who got the grudge You ain't gotta be Home Alone I ya residence*

*For me to kick ya door down, searchin' for Dead Presidents Bag up the dough and I'll be Gone in 60 Seconds*

*Come back with the Gremlins who know for clappin' them weapons Damn... Ain't that a Low Down Dirty Shame*

*They set ya Man on fire, he feelin' Major Payne Listen... I stay strapped and I'll let the heat spin ya Cause this AK got more kick than 3Ninjas*

*And... I Got the Hook Up wit' mean OGs*

*And my blow make the dope fiends Lean on Me*

*If you try trespassing, I'ma burst these poles bitch I'll turn 13 Ninjas to 13 Ghosts quick*

*Like Terminator, Bulletface know to keep a gun in hand So ya Final Instinct should be to do The Running Man'*

Birdman's eyes were wide with shock. Ricky Rozay's brows were raised high in disbelief. Standing around the two hip-hop moguls, their YMCMB and MMG recording artists seemed just as stunned.

They were all bunched together in a second floor room at the Versace mansion, a room that had once been a bedroom but was now a music studio. Blake and Alexus sat in white leather swivel chairs at the sound table. By now it had been confirmed that Young-D was in fact dead, but Meach was alive and in critical condition at the University of Miami Hospital.

The promethazine with Codeine and Sprite mixture in Blake's double-stacked Styrofoam cups had him tilted back in his chair. And the cigarillo full of OG Kush in his other hand had him on Mars. He was fighting off the emotional pain and guilt he felt over Young-D's death.

They'd been friends since kindergarten, had stayed to themselves all throughout elementary school and up until they started selling drugs in middle school. Then they started their clique of young dope boys—the Dub

Life Goonz—and they'd sold crack from then until Blake became a millionaire.

Blake only halfway noticed the shocked expressions surrounding him. He filled his lungs with smoke, took a sip of Lean, and listened to the second verse of "My Movie," the fifth track on his new mixtape.

*'I got a Black Mask and a Full Metal Jacket Act Foolish you'll get found in Lake Placid My Shottas Set It Off, you'll be dying for real Cause it's a time to chill and A Time To Kill*

*I keep the Tommy Boy, and I grip the two Tecs well Hand over your grille, have you Waitin' To Exhale*

*Look... and I'ma Die Hard wit' a four-fifth and a choppa, too Catchin' me slippin', sorry, dat Mission Impossible*

*Cause these two Glocks'll have y'all slumped in Dumpsters Both of 'em stupid, I call 'em Dumb and Dumber*

*It's all Goodfellas, Bring It On, Catch Me If You Can Clap ya mans till he quiet, nigga, Silence of the Lamb I keep steel on me like I-Robot*

*So if you Undercover Brother, you's a Psycho Cop You'll See Fire In The Sky, I BAPS 'em all*

*Wit' the chrome Fantastic Four, so Don't Be a Menace'*

"Man, is y'all hearin' this shit?" Meek Mill exclaimed. "This nigga made a song usin' the names of movies!"

"You go hard like my son," Birdman said, giving Bulletface a slap on the shoulder. "This some of the coldest shit I done heard."

"Definitely, young nigga," Ross added.

Alexus nodded solemnly. "You can dedicate this to Young-D. It'll be your second mixtape to go platinum. I'm sure of it."

"Can't believe my lil nigga dead," Bulletface muttered, passing the blunt to Rick Ross. Young-D's death was the only thing on his mind.

Rozay and Baby promised to have their guys in Miami look into the shooting, but Blake didn't need their help. He may not have known who the

shooters were, but he knew who'd sent them. There was no question about that.

They filed out of the studio soon thereafter and headed outside.

Blake had initially planned a grand party celebrating his mixtape release, but now he wanted to be alone with Alexus.

The two of them stood on the front steps, in the exact spot where the late Gianni Versace was shot dead in 1997, and bid farewell to the YMCMB and MMG millionaires.

"I had Enrique take Melonie and Tamera shopping on Collins Avenue, gave him my black card and told him to spend at least a mill on them. That'll keep their mouths shut about what happened in Matamoros," Alexus said. She moved down a step, turned to face Blake, and interlaced her fingers with his. "We've got forty armed men here with us now—ten inside the mansion, ten surrounding it, ten out there on Ocean Drive, and ten more positioned on 11th. We're good and safe, okay? No worries."

"Knew I should've bulletproofed that car."

"Don't blame yourself for this. You've never had a problem or a threat here in Miami. There's no way you could've known that T-Walk would strike here."

"I knew he lived here. I knew that I had just threatened the fuck nigga this mornin'. I know I shot his closest man's bitch. That's enough, ain't it?" Something occurred to Blake before Alexus had time to reply. His eyes became stringent slits. "You heard from your cousin lately?"

"Which cousin?"

"Don't play stupid, Alexus. You know who the fuck I'm talkin' about. That nigga Bookie. Tasia's boyfriend. What kinda car he got?"

"I don't know. Think he still has the white Jaguar I bought him a few years ago. Why? You think it was him?"

"He on Instagram?"

"Yeah, I'm pretty sure he's still on there."

"Let me see your phone," Blake said, watching Birdman's red Bugatti pull away from the curb as he turned and headed back into the mansion. Alexus fell in step beside him. "If I find out that nigga had anything to do with this shit..."

He didn't complete the threat. Didn't need to.

"You can't kill my cousin, Blake. He may be a cokehead, but he's still my uncle's son. As soon as I can locate T-Walk, you can take out all your anger on him, okay? Now— there are nine

97

luxurious bedrooms in this place. Which one do you wanna break in first?"

Blake shook his head, taking out his smartphone. He tapped into the Instagram app and went straight to Alexus's page while she pulled him into a bedroom. He quickly found Bookie's IG page; Alexus had millions of Instagram followers, but there were only fifty-six people lucky enough to have her as a follower, and Bookie was one of them.

Alexus leaned in for a kiss, but Blake pushed her onto the bed she'd just led him to. Sex was not on his mind at the moment. He was far too focused on the very first photo on Bookie's page.

It was a red car. A 745 BMW.

Blake went to his call log and dialed Mocha's number.

## *Chapter 30*

T-Walk answered his door wearing a heavy blue robe with a large six-point star and the letters GD stitched into the back of it in black thread. Over a hundred carats of blue diamonds gleamed in the platinum necklace on his neck. He wore a scowl, had an AR-15 assault rifle in his right hand and a Samsung smartphone in his left.

Bookie and Craig were on the other side of the door when T-Walk opened it. The two of them barged past him and into the extravagant suite, clad in all black — hoodies, loose-fitting jeans, and Jordan sneakers. T- Walk locked the door behind them.

"Big salute to you niggas," T-Walk said, turning and resting the top of the assault rifle on his shoulder. He watched Bookie and Craig collapse onto the blue Italian leather sofa. "Did y'all get him good? I saw it on the news."

"Good ain't the word," Craig said, lighting a Newport. "I let damn near the whole clip ride on them niggas. Got that fuck nigga Young D, too. You should've saw how he was tryna duck and dodge in the passenger seat."

"What about Blake?'

"We hit him up good, too. He was drivin'." "You sure y'all got him?"

"Yeah, I'm sure. Kinda question is that?"

"A smart one," T-Walk said, and tossed his smartphone to Craig.

While Bookie dumped a bag of cocaine on the coffee table and rolled up a hundred-dollar bill to get his hourly fix, Craig perused the breaking news T-Walk had just found on his CNN app.

"Young D and Meach?" Craig exclaimed with his brows furrowed together in disbelief.

"That's what the fuck I said," T-walk snapped. Grinding his teeth together, he dug in one of his robe's deep pockets and pulled out the key to his ocean-blue Lamborghini Aventador. He threw it at Craig's chest. "You

smart motherfuckas shot the wrong nigga. I got a half million in a duffle in the Lambo. Y'all can have that, but I'm not paying a cent more until *Bulletface* is dead."

"What?!" Bookie snatched the smartphone out of Craig's hand

and read the article himself. Then he pulled out his own smartphone to investigate further. "Maaan, this some bullshit. Can't believe this shit.

Damn. Thought we had that nigga."

"Well," T-Walk said, walking over and retrieving his phone from Bookie, "I hate to break it to you, but you thought wrong. Bulletface didn't get shot. How did y'all not know whether or not he was in the car? Y'all didn't look?"

"*This* nigga"—Bookie jabbed a thumb at Craig –"Said he saw Blake in the car." He leaned forward and snorted from the pile of coke, shaking his head in the process.

"I thought it was him," Craig argued. "Shit, he damn near look like Young Meach. They're both dark skinned, both got waves and shit. Can't blame me for making a mistake. I want that nigga dead just as bad as you do. He shot me in the wrist, shot bruh"—he returned a thumb to bookie— "in his ankle. Don't even trip though. We'll catch him one day."

"*One* day? Nah, he gets it *today*. That nigga done shot all three of us. I'm not allowing him to walk around Miami, drive around Miami—none of that. This nigga killed *Tasia* this morning. *Tasia*! And let's not forget about K.G., Johnny, Steve, and all the other bodies he's dropped. Not to mention the email I got a few hours ago saying I'm fired from Costilla Corp. you know what that means? That means no more millions for me unless I go back to the dope game, and I'll be damned if I do that." T-Walk was livid. He began pacing to and fro, fearing that at any moment Blake would burst through the door, blasting at every man in sight.

There was also a bit of jealousy in T-Walk's heart, though he'd never admit it to Craig and Bookie. Knowing that Blake had once again won over Alexus had T-Walk steaming. He wanted Blake dead as soon as possible, and he was willing to do whatever it took to get it done.

Craig said, "We gotta lay low for now. I don't want nobody seeing me in my car and pointing it out as the car the shots came from. And besides, we ain't gon' be able to catch that nigga slippin' out here. We don't even know where to find him."

T-walk stopped pacing. A wicked smile grew on his face. "Thunder!" he shouted. "Bring our friend out here."

100

Viewing Bookie and Craig's shocked reactions as thunder brought out the young woman who'd arrived moments earlier put an even wider smile on T-walk's face.

The woman was Mercedes Costilla, Alexus's sister.

"I don't think we'll have a problem finding Blake," T-Walk said.

King Rio

## *Chapter 31*

"They're letting us leave the police station in a few minutes. Oh, my god, Blake. I'm literally still shaking. I've never in my life heard so many gunshots. This is the second time I've had to go through this, Blake. First it was the incident in Chicago last year when these guys shot up your other Bugatti while I was driving it, and now this. I can't do this. I truly can't.

I'm afraid for my life now. Something has to be done about these attacks."

"I know, Mocha. Just relax a bit. I'm not happy about this shit, either, okay. And trust me; I'm already working on getting it all settled so we can continue up this road of success. Now, I need you to give me a simple yes or no answer. The red car—was it a 745 BMW?"

"Yes."

"You didn't tell that to the cops, did you?" "No."

"Okay. Good. When y'all leave the police station, drive straight here to the Versace mansion in Miami Beach."

"What's the address?"

"1116 Ocean Drive. It's safe here, a'ight? We'll kick it here for the day, and tomorrow after the video shoot we'll fly back to Chicago. I'm canceling the mixtape release party."

"Alright. I'll call you back," Mocha said, and ended the call.

Blake pocketed his phone, roving his eyes over Alexus' ravishing curves as she lay nude on the bed before him. She was on her stomach, the side of her pretty face sunken in a black and gold pillow, her loving green eyes studying Blake's indecipherable expression.

He stared at her massive butt cheeks while he tried to figure out how to end his beef with T-walk once and for all.

"That car," Alexus said. "It belongs to my cousin, doesn't it?"

Blake sat down, swiped a hand down his face, then used the same hand to reach back and rub Alexus' ass. He didn't feel like talking; he felt like doling out some retaliatory gunshots.

"Don't let your anger think for you," Alexus prudently advised. "My cousin's a fucking coke addict. Even if he was one of the shooters, he's no factor. I'll cut off his supply, and I'll bet you a new G6 that he'll be crawling back to us within the week. T-

103

walk's the real problem. I can't believe that high-yellow bastard kidnapped king. After all the things I've done for him, you know what I mean? I loved him like I love you. I gave him millions like I gave you millions, and he wants to betray *me*? All along it's been *him* who kidnapped our son? Nuh uh, I'm not going for that. He'll think I'm *Jenny* Costilla when I get done with his ass."

The side of Blake's mouth rose in a skeptical grin, and he turned to stare into the sexy green eyes he loved so much. He realized then that he loved Alexus dearly, but he did not trust her. How could he? Bookie and Craig were two of the shooters who'd gunned him down, shooting him a total of ten times, on Christmas Eve a few years ago, and T-walk had ordered the hit – all out of jealously over Alexus.

Now it was like déjà vu.

T-walk was sending his hittas at Blake, just like he'd done before. "If you ever fuck that nigga again," Blake warned, still kneading

Alexus rotund bottom, "I'm goin' back to the old me and fucking every bad bitch I see. On King Neal."

"You don't ever have to worry about me cheating." Alexus get to her knees behind him and started lifting his shirt, but he declined her sexual advance and stood up. She grabbed her hips and frowned. "Don't get mad at me, Blake. I'm not against you, okay. We're in this together. An attack on you is an attack on me."

"Yeah?" Blake wasn't convinced. "A'ight, since you're with me, tell me where to find T-walk. You *gotta* know where he lives. You lived here with that nigga. Where the fuck he at?"

Alexus hesitated. "I'm really not sure. He and I stayed here a few times," she said finally. "And I believe he had a penthouse at the

Fontainebleau Hotel."

"Ain't that hotel somewhere around here?"

"Enrique's going to take care of this. You don't need to go out for anything, Blake. Get your black ass in this bed and give me some of that big snake you got in your—"

"You tryna save that nigga," Blake said thoughtfully. "No, I am not. If anything, I'm trying to save *you*."

"Yeah, right." Blake was already backing out of the bedroom.

"I'll be right back."

He got a key to an SUV from one of the bodyguards, grabbed the duffle bag he'd packed in Mexico from the family room, and was out the door a moment later.

A quick Google search gave him the Fontainebleau's location. Turns out it was only a few blocks away.

King Rio

## *Chapter 32*

It always surprised T-Walk just how much Mercedes looked like Alexus. They were both dime piece redbones with sparkling green eyes, long black hair, and Tahiry-like derrieres. Mercedes was definitely a boss chick like her sister. She had on a white jumpsuit and red-bottomed heels. Diamonds glistened on her neck and wrists. Her hair and nails were perfectly done.

"Damn, you's a bad bitch," Craig said to Mercedes. "Look just like your sister, too."

"Don't call that bitch my sister," Mercedes snapped. "My mom is dead because of Alexus. My baby daddy is dead because of Blake. As far as I'm concerned, it's fuck both of them. Aunt Jenny should cut off their damn heads, too."

T-Walk chuckled. "Why are you here, Mercedes? You called me and said you could set Blake up for me. How do you plan on doing that? And what's the catch?"

"There is no catch. I just want somebody to fuck him up. I'm sure I can get Alexus to tell me where they're staying but I don't think I'll even need to do that. They're probably right here in Miami Beach, at that Versace mansion over on Ocean Drive."

"This is what we'll do then," T-walk said, pacing and speaking authoritatively. "Mercedes, you drive past the mansion first. Let me know if you see Alexus' security team standing outside. If they're around, Alexus is too."

"And if she's there?"

"Get her and Blake to step out in the open somewhere. Then give me a call. We'll pull up and let him have it."

"Using who's car?" Craig inquired. "Definitely not mine. I'm leaving mine here for a few days."

T-Walk nodded his head. Squinted. Tugged at the hairs on his chin. All eyes were on him. Ashley was sitting on the arm of the sofa, rolling a

blunt while gawking at her wealthy man. Mercedes was next to her, hands on hips, attention on T-Walk. Craig and Bookie were on the sofa with their submachine guns on their laps.

"I'll have us a car here in thirty minutes. Somethin' straight

107

out the hood in Miami. Mercedes, all you have to do is get Blake out in the open. *I'm* shooting him at point-blank range, and I don't care if I spend the rest of my life in prison over it. Ash, go and grab the brief cases."

T-Walk's eyes moved to the jiggling mounds of meat in the back of Ashley's tight-fitted denim short-shorts, while the eyes of his guests widened in wonder.

When Ashley returned seconds later with two steel briefcases, T-Walk set them on the glass-top coffee table, displayed a brilliant smile, and then opened them to show all the cash they held.

"I made *a lot* of drug money when I was with Alexus, and I still have about seventy million in unlaundered cash. Got two mill in each of them briefcases," T-Walk said, his smile widening as Ashley stepped out of the bedroom with another two briefcases. She made three more trips to the bedroom she and T-Walk shared, and soon there were eight steel briefcases on the floor behind him. "As long as Blake is dead before he can leave Florida, Mercedes, you've got ten million, and Bookie and Craig, you two will also have ten million. Y'all with me?"

They all were.

## *Chapter 33*

Alexus put on a white two-piece bikini and went to the outdoor pool for a relaxing swim, because swimming always managed to settle her thoughts when they were troubled.

And today, her thoughts were most certainly troubled.

The fear of Aunt Jenny had Alexus on edge. She anticipated even more wide spread terror attacks if Jenny ever get her hands on the submarines, and she was worried that Jenny's next video would be the macabre murder and beheading of someone close.

Alexus was also afraid that Blake had just left to kill her cousin Bookie. She'd been hoping to calm Blake down enough to talk him out of retaliating in response to the highway shooting, but she knew from experience that Blake never let anything slide. He was probably riding around with one of his guns at that exact moment, anxious to start bombing on whichever of his enemies he caught first.

Backstroking her way through the cool water, gazing up at the sun and the clear blue sky and the unmoving palm trees that surrounded most of mansion, Alexus struggled to come up with a solution to her overwhelming burden of worries. When none came, she shut her eyes and prayed.

*God, I ask that you please watch over my family and protect us from that crazy aunt of mine. Bless the families of all those killed in the D.C bombing and the Mexico bombings, and keep Aunt Jenny from gaining the opportunity to do it again. God, I ask that you keep Blake safe, keep Young-Meach alive, and wrap your arms around Young D's family and friends in this time of grief. Help me and Blake mend that bond we used to have. Make our love stronger than ever; and if he's not the one for me, please stop procrastinating and send me my knight in shining armor. I'd appreciate a handsome black man, no specific complexion, just an honest,*

*compassionate man who will love me and my son until the end of time. In Jesus' name I pray, Amen.*

Just then, a powerful splash at the other end of the pool interrupted Alexus' peaceful swim.

She opened her eyes and was surprised to see her mother, Rita Mae Bishop, standing beside the pool with Attorney Bostic and Neal Miller.

And swimming toward Alexus was the most handsome guy she'd ever laid eyes on.

The first thing she noticed was his smile and his shoulder-length dreadlocks. Then she took in the caramel- brown face behind the dreads, and the muscle-filled arms that were propelling him towards her. He had tattoos all over his arms and hands, and a few more on his upper chest.

"Talked them into flying straight here," Britney said, beaming. But Alexus barely heard the voice of her cheerful lawyer, because suddenly the stranger in her pool was right in front of her.

"Your mom pushed me in the water, I swear," he said, smiling "It's no big deal." Alexus gave him an equally bright smile. She reached out and shook his hand. "I'm Alexus Costilla... and you are?"

"Patrick McClure, but you can just call me Pat, or Manchild. A lot of my family calls me Manchild. I'm one of your biggest fans, believe it or not. I go nuts every time I see you on TV. All my niggas do, too. You are like the most beautiful girl in the world. I couldn't believe it when Neal said he used to date your mom. Thought for sure he was lying."

Alexus was awestruck. Speechless. Manchild had the face of a model and the physique of an NBA star. His Voice was as warm as his smile, and Alexus was tempted to test the warmth of his flesh.

"Let me... show you all inside," she stuttered, and climbed out of the pool.

## *Chapter 34*

*'Smokin' on this Compton, but bitch I'm Chiraq*
*Wherever you disrespect me at, bitch that's where you die at All these fuckin' lab rats, now I got my mouse trap*
*Niggas wanna fake kick it, wanna know where my house at That life I ain't bout that, I'm bout pushin' scalps back*
*Pull up on yo' block bitch, let my niggas air out that*

The drumming bass of Chief Keef's "War" banged from the big white Tahoe's speakers. Its sound system had been connected to an iPod full of Spanish songs when Blake got in it; but now it was connected to his iPhone, which had more Chief Keef tracks downloaded than any other artist.

Blake was parked with his hazard lights on across the street from the Fontainebleau Hotel, right in the middle of the affluent Collins Avenue.

He'd been there numerous times before, mostly for shows and parties at Club LIV, and twice with a sexy dark-skinned woman named Ebanee.

He glanced at the multimillion dollar boats that lined the Rocket Boat Tours dock to the right of him, and then went back to gazing across traffic at the Fontainebleau.

Tall and wide and grayish white, with big blue windows and swimming pools on balconies, the hotel was the absolute finest Miami Beach had to offer, a place of refuge for the rich and famous when they wanted to find the best pool parties in the land.

So seeing a clean white Maybach Landaulet convertible pulling away from the hotel did not immediately grab Blake's attention. It took the shock of watching a red BMW pull out behind it for him to give the Maybach a second look. The name on the Maybach's rear plate— MERCEDES—revealed its owners identity. Blake had seen the car too many times to count. He knew it belonged to Mercedes Costilla.

There was a Glock .45 with a 30-round clip under Blake's seat. It had come from the bodyguard who'd given him the keys to the SUV.

He grabbed the gun, turned off the hazard lights, and busted a

111

U- turn in the middle of traffic to get behind the BMW. His second iPhone5 was vibrating atop the Louis Vuitton duffle on the passenger seat, but he wasn't about to answer it. He wasn't even going to *look* at the phone.

Not until he took care of the red BMW.

## *Chapter 35*

Craig lit another cigarette.

"So, listen, we'll follow you to that mansion. I'll drive past it with you, then park somewhere close by and wait on T-Walk to come pick me and Bookie up in the hoopty. Then you just let us know when to pull up on that nigga," Craig said, holding his smartphone between him and Bookie with the speakerphone activated.

"Okay, nigga. Damn," Mercedes retorted. "You gon' get a bitch jammed up talkin' like this. I'll text you what's up. Just make sure you delete the damn texts, and... whatever y'all do, don't hurt Alexus. I might not like the bitch, but she's still my sister."

"You think I'ma let my cousin get hurt?" Bookie asked, seemingly appalled by the idea.

"Nigga, I don't know," Mercedes shot back. "You ain't my cousin.

Alexus and I have the same father, which puts all you niggas on her mother's side of the family on my non-family list. Bye."

She hung up abruptly.

Grinning and scratching the exposed scalp between two of his cornrows, Bookie grabbed his crotch and said, "Bitch playin' hard to get. Watch, I'ma get that bitch to give me some o' dat pussy, bruh. On Vice Lord, watch. You see how fat her ass is? *Know* she got some good pussy."

"She gon' make you pay some racks for dat pussy. I can bet money on that."

"And? I pay for pussy all the time."

With a laugh, Craig opened the text message Mercedes had just sent
him:

*'Straight shot down Collins to 11th Street then left and we're there.'*

He replied with a simple 'K', checked a sign and saw that they were

just now passing 40th Street, then reclined in his seat and started thinking about the $10 million he would be splitting with Bookie in a matter of

hours, maybe even minutes. He'd always dreamed of being a rich young hood nigga, and here lately his dreams were coming true. After splitting three 100-kilo cocaine shipments with Bookie and selling his half for

$35,000-$40,000 a brick, Craig now had well over $2 million stashed away in a sofa at his Miami home. He had diamond necklaces, rings, and watches. He had a brand new 2014 Escalade on 30" rims. His girlfriends and female siblings were all strutting around in designer dresses and shoes that had cost him thousands.

Yes, he was the man among his family and peers, and adding $5 million to his savings in a single day would make him an even bigger man.

As he was pulling to a stop at the traffic light on 26th and Collins, he spotted a dark gray Ferrari parked in front of the Lorraine Hotel. *'Nice,'* he thought.

Then his dreams were forever shattered.

## *Chapter 36*

Blake already had the passenger window rolled down when he pulled up next to the BMW; and he started shooting as soon as he saw Craig and Bookie inside it. The sound suppressor screwed into the Glock's barrel made heavy *THOOMP* sounds every time Blake squeezed the trigger. He hit Craig twice in the side of the head, gave Bookie a good eight rounds to the head and upper body, and then sped to the Triton Supermarket on 27th.

He veered into the parking lot and hopped out of the Tahoe with his duffle bag in hand.

Head down, He jogged across Collins Avenue. He heard a woman's scream from the corner of 26th and Collins, but he knew better than to look. He turned right on Indian Creek Drive and kept walking for several blocks, doing his best to appear inconspicuous in a neighborhood full of upper-class white people and high-end fashion boutiques.

He was contemplating climbing aboard a bus when a tan-colored minivan came screeching to a stop beside him.

"O.M.G! Bulletface! Oh, my God, like, I cannot believe this is happening right now. Can I take a picture?"

Blake ducked to look into the minivan. Sitting behind the wheel was a blonde white girl who looked to be in her early twenties, and a curly- haired black poodle sat on the passenger seat, hopping around in circles and looking from the driver to Blake.

Instinctively, he got in behind the dog without asking. The blonde twisted halfway out of her seat to stare at Blake, her eyes and mouth agape.

"Ohhhh, my God. Bulletface is in my van. Bulletface is in my van." She fanned her face with both hands. "I have to take a picture of this."

"If you take me to my house right now, I'll buy you a brand new

minivan. I need to get there as soon as possible: 11th and Ocean."

Blake was relieved to see the enthused Bulletface fan's hands go back to the steering wheel. She stepped on the gas. Within seconds, they were soaring down Collins... right past the red

115

BMW 745.

Blake stretched out on the seat and fixed his eyes on the ceiling. "I'll give you another twenty thousand on top of the van money if you can catch up with that white Maybach. She'll give me a ride from there. It's my sister's car."

"I'm one of your biggest fans. Name's Kendall Ashland, I'm from here in Miami Beach. I've been to *all* of your Club LIV shows, was screaming my head off at the last one. I've been to your concerts in Miami, New York City, Indianapolis, Chicago, Detroit—you name it. My sister's a big fan of yours, too. Oh, my God, you *have* to take a picture with me!"

Blake chuckled and slid a heavy rubber-banded pile of bank-new hundred-dollar bills from a front pocket of his baggy white jeans.

"No pictures this time," he said, "but I'll fly you and your sister out to my concert at the United Center this Thursday, and we can take pictures backstage, I promise. You on IG? I'll follow you back and message you on there. Or just give me your phone number."

She gave him her phone number over the scream of police sirens as a phalanx of squad cars raced by. His thumb trembled as he dialed her number into his smartphone and saved it.

"Something must have really happened back there. Sheesh," Kendall said. "Oh... there's the... yeah, that's a Maybach. There it is. Want me to honk the horn? Looks like it's turning onto 11th Street. What'd she do, put you out and make you walk? Never in a million years did I think I'd run into Bulletface, the most famous rapper there is. Oh, look, we're here on 11th and Ocean. Isn't this the Versace mansion?"

Kendall wouldn't stop chattering but Blake didn't find it annoying.

If anything, it made him like her even more. She was obviously a bright- spirited woman. Her eyes were blue and as pretty as her face. Her breasts were as large as melon and threatening to spill over the top of her halter. She had probably just saved Blake from a life in prison, and he was grateful.

"Don't honk, just stop and let me out," he said, sitting up and handing her the pile of cash. "Here you go. That's thirty thousand dollars.

Should be able to get yourself a nice new van with that. Now excuse me, but I gotta catch my sister."

The gaudy white Maybach was turning onto Ocean Drive. Blake got out and ran after it.

King Rio

## *Chapter 37*

"Your mom's talk show is family hour at my sister's house. She's like the new Oprah, only richer. Hope she plans on dishing out a few of those dollars to get me a new phone. It was in my pocket when she pushed me into that pool."

"I'll order you a new phone."

"You serious? Wait till I tell my hood niggas about this. They ain't even gon' believe me. Alexus Costilla bought me a phone. I'm keepin' that phone forever." Patrick raised the right side of his mouth in a gentle grin.

Alexus couldn't help but to smile. She was laid back on a big white lounge chair next to the outdoor swimming pool, nursing an ice-cold glass of Hennessey and Pepsi through a straw and scrolling though Instagram.

Honestly, she was only looking at her phone to keep from gawking at Manchild, who was sitting up in the lounge chair beside her wearing nothing but a bath towel that was wrapped around his waist. He was tall—at least 6'4"—and he was covered in tattoos from neck to waist. He reminded Alexus of the rapper Waka Flocka.

Alexus loved Waka Flocka.

"Mind if I ask you a... personal question?" said Manchild.

"Feel free."

"Is your butt real?"

Alexus snickered. "Yes. I'm all natural. Got all this junk in my trunk from my momma."

"I knew it was real. Just had to ask. My nigga Baby Mike always satin' it's fake, but I knew it wasn't. It looked too real in that Bulletface "Lime Green Bugatti" video. I saw that muhfucka jiggle and *knew* it was real. On the hood. Had me wantin' to kiss the TV."

"You are somethin' else." Alexus laughed again.

"How long you think it's gon' be before my clothes dry?"

"Why? You afraid of wearing a towel in front of me?"

"*Hell* nah. I'm just not a pervert. Give me the word and I'll snatch this muhfucka right off."

"Oh, believe me, if Blake and I weren't trying to fix our relationship, I'd have already gotten you out of that towel."

"Who is Blake?" "Bulletface."

"Aw... I thought he was fuckin' wit' Mocha. Saw 'em holdin' hands on 106$^{th}$ and Park a few weeks ago."

"Holding hands with Mocha?" Alexus showed a petulant scowl. She hadn't heard anything about Blake holding Mocha's hand.

Seconds later, she was on YouTube, searching for the video. She found it in no time, and sure enough, there Blake was, sitting on the 106$^{th}$ and Park couch hand-in-hand with Mocha, revealing to Bow-Wow the list of recording artists that would be featured on his upcoming album.

"Hmm," Alexus said, "I hadn't seen this."

"Damn. Hope I didn't just get the homie jammed." Manchild laughed and shook his dreads. "I fucks wit' Bulletface and the whole MBM. Them niggas takin' over like Cash Money. He showed out last time he came to Nap, through like a hundred racks at Pure Passion. The strippers love that nigga; all the dope boys love that nigga. He's like Yo Gotti mixed wit' Chief Keef, and the nigga got that Diddy bread. A muhfucka can't even hate on that."

Maybe it was the Hennessey surging through Alexus' bloodstream, or maybe it was because deep down she wanted to be angry at Blake so she wouldn't feel so wrong about her attraction to Manchild, but suddenly her blood was boiling as she watched the YouTube video for the second time.

Shaking her head and rolling her eyes indignantly, she set the smartphone down on her thigh and turned to finally acknowledge Manchild.

"Bulletface is just plain, old cheating ass Blake to me," Alexus said, taking another sip of her drink. "I wouldn't be a bit surprised if he is

fucking that bitch."

Manchild let out a triple "ha" laugh, and then eased back in his fluffy lounge chair, interlacing his fingers behind his head and casting an open-mouthed smile at the sky. Police sirens blared from somewhere nearby.

"Still can't believe I'm sitting here poolside with Alexus. This shit is blowing my mind." He looked over at her, and for a couple seconds he said nothing; then, ""You heard about Young-D and

Meach? We heard some people at the airport talkin' about it. They say Young-D didn't make it. I hate to hear that. I like his music."

"Yeah. It is sad. What's even sadder is that Blake's stupid ass is going to shoot somebody about it first chance he gets."

"Nah, what's sad is that auntie of yours. She *nuked* a city in the *U.S.A.*, blew up the *White House*, killed the *president*, and now she done recorded a video showing her cut off three damn heads. That shit's crazy. I bet they end up shootin' her in the head when they catch her; same way they did bin Laden. She ain't even gotta be a threat and they still gon' blast her ass. I wonder where she's at."

"You're not the only one wondering that," Alexus said, her eyes glued to Manchild's six-pack.

She felt her pussy getting wetter and wetter by the second. Her nipples were stiff behind the sheer bikini top. She wanted to mount him on that chair, take his towel off, push her panties to the side, and…

"Alexus!" Britney shouted as she came running out of the mansion in a panic. "Blake is out front with Mercedes, and he's got a gun to her head!"

King Rio

## *Chapter 38*

"What the fuck is up wit' this bitch?!" Blake snapped as soon as Enrique and Britney returned with Alexus.

He was standing in the foyer behind Mercedes Costilla with a Glock pressed to the back of her head. His face was a mask of fire, and the submachine guns Enrique's men were aiming at him only added fuel to the flames.

Mercedes was sobbing uncontrollably with her face buried in her hands.

"Jesus Christ, Blake! My mom is in this house somewhere!" Alexus

said, motioning for her security team to lower their weapons. "Why do you a fucking gun pointed at the back of my sister's head? What's going on?"

"I'm sorry," Mercedes said through tears. "I'm… I'm sorry Alexus.

I'm sorry Blake. I shouldn't have went to see him. It's just that I'm broke now. I'm broke and depressed, and he promised to put me back on my feet if I could set up Blake for him."

"Wait a minute—What?" Alexus grabbed her hips.

Hearing the confession from Mercedes did not exactly extinguish Blake's fiery anger, but it did calm him down a bit. He picked up his duffle from the marble floor and handed the Glock to Enrique. Get rid of that for me. ASAP. And send somebody to pick up that Tahoe I borrowed. Left it at the supermarket on 27th and Collins."

"Is that why there's a hundred cop cars down there?"

Blake ignored the inquiry and turned back to Mercedes. "Go ahead, Mercedes. Tell her what you told me in the car."

"I blew the money you gave me on my husband, and now he's locked up in Gary, Indiana for a double-murder that happened before he and I even met. They found over a hundred kilos of dope in our house when they raided it looking for him. That led to the feds seizing everything—the mansion, our cars, the jet, our bank accounts. Kenny took the blame for the drugs, but both of our names was on all the paperwork for everything that

was seized so there's no getting any of it back. Luckily, I had just took the Maybach in for new tires and an oil change, or I

123

would've lost that, too."

Mercedes wiped her eyes again, sniffled and sailed on.

"I've been so depressed lately. My husband's in jail. The father of my kids is dead. I went from being a millionaire one day to pawning jewelry the next day. When T-Walk called and offered me millions to help him... kill Blake...I couldn't turn it down. Bookie and Craig were following me here to do it. I was supposed to get Blake out in the open so they could kill him."

"And where are Craig and Bookie now? Alexus asked.

"I don't know. They were right behind me on Collins and I was texting Craig. Then he stopped replying and a bunch of police cars started popping up with their lights and sirens on. I'm so sorry, Alexus. Please... forgive me."

Mercedes broke down crying again. This time, Alexus stepped forward and hugged her, giving her a shoulder to cry on and rubbing her back.

Blake stared at Alexus' bikini bottom and the meaty cheeks it exposed, suddenly wishing he would have taken her up on her offer to relieve some stress before he'd left in search of his enemy.

"I'm your sister," Alexus murmured. "You could've called me.

Money means nothing; family means everything. If I have it, you have it. All you have to do is ask."

Alexus turned and regarded Blake through tightly squinted eyes. "What?" He grinned.

"You know what. Did you see Bookie following her?"

His grin deepened. "I ain't seen nobody, baby. Ask your sister who shot my niggas, though. And they were tryin' to shoot *me*. Fuck them niggas."

Blake turned to leave the foyer, deciding it was best to lay in a bed somewhere and think over his next move.

But then he found himself face-to-face with a tall, dreadlocked man in a towel.

"The fuck? Put some muhfuckin' clothes on nigga. Who you here wit'?" The words raced out of Blake's mouth.

"Rita pushed me in the pool with Alexus when we got—" The guy didn't get a chance to finish voicing his explanation. Blake's fist slammed into his jaw and knocked him out cold.

124

## Chapter 39

Enrique chuckled dryly. Alexus and Britney gasped in unison. And suddenly Mercedes sobbing spell ended.

"You got naked niggas all in the pool when I'm gone? What kinda shit is that?" Blake asked. Sheer disbelief raised his voice an octave above its normal pitch. His brows furrowed at Alexus as she grabbed his wrist.

"Let's go to the bedroom, Blake. Right now. Enrique, get that boy to a hospital and then a hotel. They're not about to tear my house down fighting when he wakes up."

"Nah," Blake said, snatching out of Alexus' grasp. "I'm good. I'm done talkin'. Talk to your boyfriend. I'm gone."

"Don't do this to me, Blake." This time Alexus curled the fingers of both her hands around his wrist, and her eyes got watery. "I cannot lose you again, okay? Please, let's just go talk. We'll get all this sorted out. You don't have to leave."

Blake was just about to rip free again and storm out the front door when his favorite lawyer squeezed his shoulder and whispered in his ear. "Go with her, Blake. You know how much she loves you. Just go talk with her. Don't blame anyone but me for bringing that guy here."

Reluctantly, he let Alexus pull him to the bedroom they visited earlier. There were two large walk-in closets with adjoining bathrooms, and across from the foot of the bed was a vast room with sofas and flatscreen televisions. Alexus pushed Blake onto the sofa and mounted him.

"You're crazy, you know that? Ape-shit fucking crazy," she said, holding his face in her hands. "You did not have to hit him like that."

"Fuck I look like lettin' a nigga walk around my girl wearin' nothin' but a towel? This ain't that. Lucky I didn't shoot that nigga."

"What did you do to Craig and Bookie?"

"Same thing they did to me. Same thing they did to Young-D and Meach."

"You killed my cousin?"

"Fuck yo' cousin. When T-Walk sent them niggas at me that Christmas Eve, they shot me ten times. *Ten* times. Then T-Walk almost killed me last year, and today they tried to kill me *again*. Fuck that. I'm goin' back to the old Blake. Fuck every nigga who ain't wit' me. They can all get it."

Alexus hesitated. "Were you seen?" she asked, finally.

"Shit, I don't know. I don't think so. Wasn't a lot of traffic, and the gun had a silencer on it."

"You're crazy."

"You said that already."

"Well, I'm saying it again. You're crazy. Crazy, crazy, fucking crazy."

"No, I'm just smart enough to shoot first. You seen how Pac and

Biggie got killed. Doe-B got killed not too long ago. Nigga shot at Rozay right here in Miami. Be damned if I let a fuck nigga smoke me. Soon's I catch that nigga T-Walk, I'm knockin' his hat off, too."

Alexus sighed and shook her head despondently, while Blake rubbed her thighs and sniffed for what he thought he'd just smelled on her breath.

"I think we should get out of the country for a little while," she said.

"I'm not runnin' from nothin', Alexus. I got shows to do. You can go wherever you wanna go, but I'm goin' right back to Chicago after the Magic City party tomorrow."

"And I'm going with you." "You been drinkin'?"

"A little. Just some Henny and a soda. You had me too stressed out when you left. I went for a swim and then had a drink."

"Wit' that fuck nigga?"

"No, Blake. Momma pushed him into the pool as a joke. He was only wearing the towel because his clothes are in the dryer."

"Mmm hmm," Blake grunted skeptically.

"I wouldn't lie to you about something this serious. We were just sitting by the pool chit-chatting."

"About what?"

Alexus sucked her teeth. "About you holding hands with Mocha on 106th and Park. What the hell was that about? You fuckin' her?"

126

"Glad I did knock that nigga out," Blake chuckled as he moved forward and lightly bit her left breast through the fabric of her bikini top, while the fingers of his hand sank between her succulent brown thighs and massaged the center of them.

"Answer the question, Bulletface." She pushed his shoulder, nibbling the corner of her bottom lip. A barely audible moan crawled halfway out of her throat.

"I have never fucked Mocha, okay? I wanted to at one time, but I never have. Honestly."

"Stop," Alexus moaned. "You know what you're doing to me."
"You lock the door?"

"Of course I did." "You want this dick?"

"Of course I do," Alexus exhaled breathlessly.

Blake could feel the juices soaking through her bikini bottom. He slid it to the side and dug a middle finger into her wet, warm hole, freeing her perky breasts from the bikini top with his teeth. His foot-long phallus was erect and pressing against the zipper of his cash-filled True Religion jeans. Alexus lifted the heavy gold and diamond MBM pendant that hung from his equally weighty gold necklace. He grinned to show the diamonds on his teeth.

"Hey look," he said, and glanced at his blinging watch, "I need some guns. Gotta make a few calls before I deal with you."

"All my men have guns, Blake. No one's coming in here without getting gunned down first." Alexus kneeled before him and undid his Louis Vuitton belt. "Plus, I have guns in both our closets. You haven't even looked yet."

She tugged his dick out of his boxers and immediately sucked its head into her mouth. Blake dropped his head back and closed his eyes as Alexus' rhythmic sucking began. Police sirens were screaming as squad cars sped past behind the mansion, but the only sounds that mattered to Blake at the moment were the slurps he heard every time the crown of his dick hit the back of Alexus' throat.

"Mmm. This dick tastes so good," she said while still sucking him.

Blake opened his eyes and grinned at her. "That Henny gotchoo on beast mode, I see. I love when you get like this. Eat it up."

And that she did. In fact, she fellated him so expertly that he

127

wondered who she'd been practicing on over the past year. She jerked and twisted and squeezed his long black pole with her hands, sucking and licking it, slapping it on her tongue and lips, and then deep-throating it over and over again until Blake could no longer take it.

He yanked his dick out from between her thirsty sucking lips and stood up. "You gon' be done made me nut before you even get yours off," he said, picking her up from her kneeling position on the floor and bending her over the sofa. He untied her bikini bottom and rubbed her lubricious pussy as it dropped to the floor.

"Don't play with me, Blake. I'm too tipsy for all that." "You think I'm about to play with you? Do I ever play?" "Just fuck me."

Blake wasted no time in honoring her request. He enjoyed hearing Alexus gasp as he buried a good ten of his twelve inches inside her, and her gasps grew into passionate moans seconds later. She arched her back and

massaged her clit. Blake pulled a thirty-thousand-dollar bundle of bank-new hundreds out of a front pocket, then pushed his jeans and boxers down and hastened his thrusts.

"This what you askin' for?" he said. "Am I playin' now? Huh?" "Noooooooo."

"That's what I thought."

Blake's signature grin returned. He took the rubber bands of his cash bundle, ripped off the $10,000 bank wraps, and started thumbing the bills off the pile.

Crisp green Benjamins rained down on Alexus' wildly undulating ass.

## *Chapter 40*

"I love you, Rita Mae Bishop. I've loved you ever since I laid eyes on you, when you bashed me with the driver's door of that U-Haul truck." Neal chuckled and tapped his lips against hers.

The two of them were naked beneath red-and-gold Versace sheets in the king-size bed of a second-floor bedroom. Neal was on top of Rita. His penis was flaccid inside the semen-filled condom, but he was not in a hurry to remove it from Rita's tight, creamy center; especially not while her vaginal muscles were still contracting in orgasm.

"Oh... I needed that... I needed that so much," she said, breathing heavily.

"We both needed it. I'm hoping to get a lot more of it in the future." "Shut your mouth and get off of me, you crazy man."

Neal Miller let out a second chuckle as he rolled onto his back.

"This is my first time having sex since Jenny's men killed Frederick last year," Rita said.

"Jenny won't be living much longer. She'll be dead as soon as our troops find her. You can count on that."

"God will punish her for the crimes she's committed against humanity. I really want to hate that woman for all the pain she's brought into my life, but then I'd be no better than her. God says we should forgive. Love thy neighbor. He'll discipline my enemies in due time."

"You've got too much faith in God. Some things are better left to men, and Jennifer is one of them."

Out of the corner of his eye, Neal saw the beautiful dark woman turn onto her side and lift herself up on her elbow to gaze at him, but he kept his eyes on the ceiling.

"There is no such thing as too much faith," she said. "What do you have if you don't have God? Jenny Costilla nailed me to a cross, Neal. A

cross. I prayed and prayed and prayed; and just when I thought I could not live another second in so much pain, He saved me."

"*Okay*, Rita Mae," Neal interjected.

Just then, someone knocked on the bedroom door. Rita jumped out of bed and ran to the bathroom. Neal got up, discarded his used condom in the trashcan, and stepped into his underwear.

"Neal? You awake in there?" It was Britney. "Yeah, gimme a sec," he responded.

"Umm…" Britney cleared her throat. "You're not going to like this.

Is Rita awake?"

Rita shouted, "I'm getting in the shower."

Tucking in his shirt, Neal opened the door and greeted the pretty- faced lawyer with a smile. "What is it?"

"It's about Patrick. He's, umm… being taken to the hospital." "The *hospital*. Christ, what happened?"

"He had an altercation with Blake. I think his jaw's broken, but he'll be okay. He was able to walk out on his own two feet with some help."

"That fucking Blake. Excuse my language, but he's an asshole." "Tell me about it." Britney shook her head. "I'll book Patrick a suite

in Miami. Obviously, he can't stay here, and I don't think he should be here in Miami Beach while Blake's here. No telling what'll happen if they cross paths again."

"That fucking Blake," Neal repeated in disbelief. "Yeah, I know."

"Neal sighed as he shut the door. He checked the bathroom and saw steam rolling up out of the shower. "I hate your son-in-law, Rita Mae, with a passion. You hear me? I don't know what Alexus sees in that boy, but all I see is trouble, one hundred percent trouble. It's no surprise that he's been shot more times than I can count on both hands. He deserved every bullet."

"Oh, Lord." Rita's sugary laughed filled the air. "What's he done now?"

Neal Miller did not reply. He was already sitting on the bed with his

phone in hand… dialing FBI Special Agent Josh Sneed's mobile number.

"You are not going to believe this," he said when Sneed answered. "Our guy was so fucking close to Alexus, and Blake King just ruined it.

Patrick's on his way to the hospital with a broken jaw." "Are

130

you saying Bulletface assaulted an FBI agent?" "That's exactly what I'm saying."

"I'll have him arrested and charged within the hour."

"No. We don't want to blow Patrick's cover, and I definitely don't want to blow mine, okay? Just give me some time. I'll get this figured out. When it's all said and done, we'll have Blake charged with the murders of those Michigan City police officers, and we'll know for certain if Alexus knows where Jenny Costilla is hiding."

"And if Alexus is in anyway tied to that Matamoros drug cartel," Sneed said before ending the call.

King Rio

## Chapter 41

Bella Costilla's body may have been stretched out on a massage table at her favorite Hollywood spa, but her thoughts were elsewhere. She'd spotted several cars following her from LAX, and now she was certain the black Altima that was creeping past her matte-black Rolls Royce Phantom was occupied by some sort of federal agent.

Studying the live video feed on the screen of her smartphone, she found herself silently thanking her Rolls Royce dealer for customizing the Phantom with panoramic cameras.

She zoomed in on the Altima driver's face. He was a young white man in sunglasses and a Dodgers cap—obvious fed.

"You guys can't do better than that?" Bella murmured, cheesing through the circular hole at the head of her massage table.

She adjusted her earpiece and dialed her father's number. "You being followed, too?" Flako immediately asked.

"That's what I was calling to tell you. They've been on me since I left the airport. Think it's about Jenny?"

"Who knows? Where's your double?"

"She's driving in from Santa Barbara, should be here any minute
now."

"Good. I'm on the flight to Venezuela, but I think I'm going to tell
the pilot to land in Colombia. Medellin, maybe. I was followed to the airport in Mexico City, and I don't want to lead anyone to Venezuela if that's where Jenny truly is."

"Why not?"

"Because then they'd kill her before I get my hands on her. She'll pay for what she did to your brother, Bella. I refuse to lose my kids the way she lost hers."

"Papi murdered Jenny's children. Can't really blame her for wanting a little payback."

"Well, she should have killed *Papi's* kid! She should have killed *Alexus*, or *Mercedes*! I've *never* done my sister wrong! It's okay, though. She'll pay for it soon enough. Lose that tail before you head out for Malibu, and keep your phone close. I love you, princess."

"Love you too, Dad."

Bella relaxed for a while and let her Asian masseuse work magic on her back. She was a Japanese immigrant who'd been oiling and rubbing Bella's body for years. She hardly knew a word of English, but she understood the few words Bella always spoke to her, and she completely understood the value of the hundred-dollar bills Bella gave her after every session.

Bella looked over at her. "Jamaica?" she said.

The masseuse toweled the oil from her hands, went to the wall phone, and dialed a number. She said, "Jamaica?" and hung up a few seconds later.

"Ten minutes," she said and continued massaging Bella's lower back.

*'I cannot wait! Bella thought,'* half-smiling as she manually typed a

number into her smartphone and hit *SEND*. It rang once, twice, thrice... and then the world's most wanted terrorist answered.

## *Chapter 42*

"My dear niece, God, how I've missed you."

Standing in front of the bathroom mirror in her small studio apartment, Jennifer Costilla studied the reflection of her gauze-wrapped head and wondered how her new face would look whenever the swelling and bruising healed. She'd gotten a full facial reconstructive surgery shortly after recording the video in Venezuela, and now here she was in Panama City, Panama, where she planned to stay until she was ready to make her return to the United States.

"I'm working on getting the ten," Bella said, "but it's going to be a difficult task. The queen's security has already tripled since the video was released, and all their orders come directly from Enrique, who gets them straight from the queen herself. Kinda hard to get around that chain of command."

"It must be done." Jenny's tone was soft and authoritative. "I'm trying my best, Aunt Je—"

"Sophia. Call me Sophia. And *trying* your best is not enough. Get it done, Bella. Get the job done. You're to just *trying* to take Alexus' place.

Are you? No, you're in the process of *doing* it, and you will succeed. Confidence is key."

"You're right."

"Am I ever wrong, my dear niece? Have I ever led you in the wrong direction? I know you're not with me in my fight against the US government, and I don't blame you for that. It's under-standable. They tortured *me* in that military prison, not you. But as your father's sister, as the daughter of your grandparents, I'm asking for your help. In return, I will help you take the throne of the family business and rise to new heights. I have faith in you, Bella. You'll be the best damn cartel boss in history, and I'm going to help you get there. We both know how soft the queen is. If she finds out that her subs were used in a second attack against the States, trust me, she will voluntarily hand over control of the cartel to you. I'd bet my life on it."

"Yeah... I hope so."

There was a pause in conversation. Jenny stepped out of the dilapidated bathroom and stared vacantly at her boyfriend Miguel, who was sitting Indian-style on a bare mattress, cleaning his AK-47. Jenny was admiring his shirtless chest when Bella spoke.

"She's with that rapper now. They're dating again." "Who, that Blake guy?" Jenny asked.

"Yeah. They're in Florida. He's her son's father." "Are his parents still around?"

"Yeah, I believe so."

"Well, there you go. Losing them will also hurt the queen. Have them killed first, then have her little rapper boyfriend killed. And remember, no *trying*. Get it done, preferably today."

## *Chapter 43*

Bella sighed as the call ended. She liked Blake. A lot. She didn't want to hurt him or his family.

But if that's what it took for her to take control of the Costilla Cartel, then she would do it with little remorse.

She called Alexus. ""Yeah," Alexus answered. "You guys still in Florida?" Alexus hesitated. "Why?"

"Just asking. My dad's on his way to Venezuela now. God I hope he finds that woman and does her the way she did my brother. I'll keep you posted. Hopefully, we'll learn something today."

"Yeah, you do that."

"What's the matter with you? I sense an attitude."

"No attitude," Alexus said. "I'm just remembering when a certain cousin of mine planted a bomb on my car at the Matamoros mansion, a bomb that would have killed me and my son had I not been arguing with Cereniti when it was detonated."

"Oh, come on, Alexus. You got me back for that." "Doesn't mean I trust you not to do it again."

"I'm mourning the loss of my brother, Alexus. I just want to hang out and talk to my cousin, my boss. Nothing more."

"Fine. I'm at the Versace mansion, 1116 Ocean Drive."

"Okay, I'll fly in later tonight. I'm too paranoid to stay here in LA. Feds are following me everywhere."

"You're being followed?"

""Yeah, my dad is too. Pedro's with him."

"Don't go to the Malibu mansion until—"

"I know, Lexi. See you later, big cousin," Bella said, adding a bit of cheer to her tone. She reached down to her white leather Gucci bag, dropped the phone in it, and lifted out a ten-inch bundle of rubber-banded hundreds just as a knock came at the door.

She turned over and sat up, already beaming, topless and arrogant with her big pile of cash. Her breaths ceased for five seconds as the masseuse opened the door and let "Jamaica" in.

Tall, dark and replete with muscles that bulged out of his finely tailored black suit, he was a stripper originally from Jamaica, hence the name. Bella had met him two months prior at a jewelry store in Denver. She'd been in town overseeing a cocaine shipment

137

and had stopped at Rika Jewelry Design to get herself a diamond tennis bracelet when Jamaica walked in looking for an inexpensive watch. "Eighteen hundred's my limit," he'd said to the jewelry dealer.

Bella had laid her black American Express card on the counter and bought him two Rolex watches for $40,000 apiece, as well as a necklace and tennis bracelet set full of diamonds for herself, and Jamaica had been hers ever since.

"I leave now," the masseuse said, walking out and shutting the door. Jamaica smiled and pulled his long dreadlocks back into a ponytail,

while Bella tossed aside the towel that had hidden the rest of her nakedness.

Fingering her gushy wet pussy and biting her lower lip, Bella raised the tall pile of cash and said, "Can you guess the dollar amount of ten inches worth of hundreds?"

"I have not a clue." Jamaica was undressing hurriedly.

"Well, you're about to find out… depending on your stamina, of course."

## *Chapter 44*

Alexus walked out the front gate behind Blake with her hands covering his eyes. "You ready?" she asked excitedly.

"Hurry up before a muhfucka ride past and shoot me," Blake replied.

She dropped her hands, and Blake gawked at the luxury car that sat at the curb. It looked like a smaller version of his triple-black Phantom convertible.

"Surprise!" Alexus beamed. "It's the new Rolls Royce Wraith, the Drophead Coupe version. The Wraith has been out for a few months now, but you're the first to have the drop-top version."

"Aw, hell yeah. I love it." Blake turned and kissed Alexus on the cheek, forcing himself to show an appreciative smile.

Honestly, he did not feel like smiling. His heart was aching over Young-D's unfortunate death, and knowing how determined T-Walk was to have him killed had him on edge.

Nervously flicking his eyes in every direction, he walked around the rear of the Wraith, got in the driver seat, and leaned toward the passenger door to open it for Alexus. She handed him the key, and he didn't utter a single word until he had the top closed and the tinted windows rolled shut.

"Thanks, baby," he finally said.

"Don't thank me. If anything I should be thanking you. You've given me a child, and I thank God for that every day." Alexus began rolling her smartphone in her lap. "She's up to something. I can *feel* it."

"What? Who the fuck are you talkin' about?"

My cousin Bella; she called she called when you were in the bedroom getting dressed, said she's flying in tonight to spend some time with me. Call it intuition, but I sensed something in her voice. Something wrong. I don't trust that bitch. She already tried to blow up me and our son in Matamoros."

"Just give me the word." Blake slipped a hand under his black-and- gold Versace shirt and eased out the gun he'd taken from the bedroom closet—a 9-millimeter Glock with a 30-round clip. "I'm done playin' games, baby. Fuck everybody. It's me and you against the world. I'm not getting shot again, and I'll be damned if I let anything happen to you or my son. Let your cousin come. She thinks it's a chess game, let her move a pawn."

"You're crazy," Alexus snickered and regarded him with a side-eyed stare. "My mom thinks you're crazy, my dad thought you were crazy, and now I'm a hundred percent certain that you are truly crazy."

"Crazy about you."

"Yeah, me and that Mocha bitch. I'm telling you now, if I ever catch you and her holding hands or doing anything other than talking—*business* talking—and making music, I'm doing her the same way you did Tasia. I'm done playing games, too. And we're getting married *this* year, no ifs, ands, or buts about it."

"I'm with that," Blake chuckled drably. "You'd better be."

"Stop talking shit 'fore I put you out my car."

Alexus rolled her eyes and smirked. She looked so unbelievably sexy doing it that Blake had to lean in and kiss the left side of her pretty lips.

"We can get married today if you want to," he said, rubbing her thigh. "I love you, Alexus. We're the 2014 Bonnie and Clyde. Who can stop us?"

"Seems like the feds may be trying to stop me. Bella said she was being followed, and she said Flako and Pedro are being followed, too."

"That means they might be following you." "Duh, smart guy."

Blake swept his eye up Ocean Drive, then stared into his side-view mirror and adjusted it a bit. He didn't see any suspicious-looking cars.

Enrique and four more bodyguards were standing around the Wraith, holding back a dozen tourist who had probably come to snap pictures of the Versace mansion but were now busy aiming their smartphone cameras at the Rolls Royce I hopes of getting a good photo of America's number one billionaire.

"Put that gun away before someone gets a picture of it," Alexus said, scrolling through Instagram. "And speaking of pictures, your mom is going selfie crazy with the kids." She laughed. "They're at Disney World."

140

"She needs to stop postin' pictures."

"Oh, please. She's got four armed bodyguards with her. There's absolutely nothing to be worried about. Now, come on, let's go back inside. Melonie and Tamera are dying to show me the clothes they got from Louis
—"

"I'm not going back in there." Alexus frowned. "Why the hell not?"

"Didn't you say your mom was upstairs with that cop? I'm not fuckin' wit' that nigga. He tried to charge me with all those murders, and locked me up for shootin' Bookie and Craig that day. I'm cool on him."

"You have to get to know him if he's dating my mom, Blake. It's not like you'll be seeing much of him today anyway. Momma ain't had a man in a whole year. She'll be enjoying him all day."

Blake was shaking his head. "Nuh-uh. Fuck that," he said.

Then a rusty old Monte Carlo came screeching off 11th street and onto Ocean Drive, plowing through the crowd of tourists. A masked man rose up out of the passenger window and aimed an AR-15 assault rifle at the windshield of Blake's brand new Wraith.

Instinctively, Blake dove toward Alexus and shielded her body with
his.

BOOM! BOOM! BOOM! BOOM! BOOM!

King Rio

## *Chapter 45*

"Grandma, do you think my daddy and Alexus are gonna stay together this time? Can you make him stay with her this time?"

"Vari, your father has a mind of his own, a mind I'll never be able to understand. Lord knows he needs to stick it out with that girl, but you just never know with Blake King."

The four of them—Dale, Carolyn, Savaria, and King Neal—were just getting off of the Buzz Lightyear's Space Ranger Spin ride and were on their way to The Haunted Mansion. They had already visited Space Mountain, Splash Mountain, the Enchanted Tiki Room, the Jungle Cruise, the Swiss Family Treehouse, and Tom Sawyer Island.

Needless to say, Carolyn and Dale were already bone-tired.

"My back is killing me," Dale complained. "Let's go to the room for a little while and rest up. It's still pretty early. We've got time to make it back and check out The Haunted Mansion."

"Aww maaaan," King Neal said, stuffing another ball of blue cotton candy in his mouth.

"No complaints, young man," Carolyn said to him. "Yeah, don't be a baby," Savaria added.

"Fuck you, bitch."

Carolyn and Dale's mouths fell open in shock, and Savaria gasped.

One of the bodyguards laughed.

Dale quickly delivered two hard slaps to King Neal's ass, bringing tear to the little boy's eyes, but he quickly wiped them away and said, "I'm tellin' my momma."

*****

Their room was at Disney's Saratoga Springs Resort and Spa, a two- bedroom villa that cost an arm and a leg but was worth every penny.

Neither of them had hardly spoken since hearing King Neal's surprising

words at the theme park, and Carolyn was ready to call his mother and do some cursing of her own as they entered the room. She balled the chest of King Neal's shirt in her fist and squatted

143

before him.

"You get your frail little behind in that bedroom this minute, you hear me? You're going to take a bath, and then you're staying in that room for the rest of the day. I don't want to *ever* hear you talking like that again. Are we clear?"

Bottom lip poked out, King Neal nodded his head, looked over at his big sister, and said, "I'm sorry, Vari."

"It's okay, brother." Savaria hugged him tightly.

Standing up, Carolyn told Savaria to go and fill the tub with warm water for King Neal's bath. She shook her head as they disappeared around a corner.

"That little boy is just as crazy as his damn daddy," she said, turning to Dale as he closed the door on their bodyguards. "I am about to call Alexus and give her a piece of my mind."

"She definitely has some explaining to —"

Something heavy suddenly thumped against the door. Dale and Carolyn froze, brows knitted together quizzically.

"Stand back, baby," Dale said, nudging her back with a forearm as he opened the door.

The four bodyguards were on the floor with bullet holes in their foreheads, and two Hispanic men wearing black bandanas over their lower faces were standing at the door. The handguns at their sides were equipped with silencers.

Carolyn witnessed her husband's brains spray out the back of his head. As she turned to flee, she saw King Neal peeking his head around the corner, his little eyes wide with fear.

"RUN!" Carolyn screamed frantically.

She felt the devastating bullets spiraling through her upper back, stinging rounds that sent her straight to the floor. The last stinging sensation was at the rear of her skull. Seconds later, Carolyn King was in heaven.

## *Chapter 46*

"Everything's okay. Come on, get out of the car," Enrique had said as he opened Alexus' door.

Blake had risen to find three bullet holes in his seat and four in his windshield; and upon stepping out of the Wraith, he'd seen at least forty holes in the Monte Carlo, which had crashed into a palm tree across the street. Alexus' men had shot it to pieces.

Enrique had then rushed Blake and Alexus into the Mercedes van and rushed them back to the airport. An hour had passed since then. Now they were 30,000 feet in the air on the Gulfstream G650, lancing toward their West Coast destination at speeds of nearly 600 miles per hour.

"Why the fuck is she not answering," Blake said as he dialed Carolyn's number for the fifteenth time. "I'm gettin' worried, baby. My momma *always* answers her phone."

"Stop saying that, Blake. I'm worrying myself to death over here." Seated across the table from him, Alexus was surfing the web on her iPhone5. "Oh, my God," she blurted out, suddenly.

"What?" Blake dropped his phone onto his lap.

"Google *'Disney World'*. Oh, my God, it says *'Eight dead in Disney World shooting.'* It's breaking news."

Blake pressed the palms of his hands to his eyes and slowly tilted his head back. *'This day cannot be happenin'*,' he thought. *'God, please let my family be okay. PLEEEEASE.'*

When he looked at Alexus a moment later, her phone was to her ear.

Tears were threatening suicide jumps along her bottom lids. There were three glasses of ice on the circular table, and Enrique was pouring Ciroc vodka over the cubes.

"Just received word from our men at the Versace mansion," Enrique said, sliding a glass to Blake. "We gave every one of those tourists ten grand apiece to keep you and Alexus out of that little incident. Both the shooter and the driver had tattoos identifying them as members of the

Gangster Disciples. Neither of them made it." He took a swallow of vodka and stepped back as Alexus walked around the table and sat on Blake's lap.

The melodious tunes of Mary J. Blige were drifting out of the overhead speakers. Blake looked out the oval window to his right and gazed vacantly into the clouds. *'Eight dead in Disney World shooting,'* he thought. Momma and Pops. Vari and King. The thoughts were almost too overwhelming to ponder.

"Yes," Alexus said, "I'm calling to check on a few of your guests; they're family members of mine. Dale and Carolyn King."

She laid her right hand on Blake's, pushed her fingers through his, and squeezed. She had it on speakerphone. Blake heard a man say he was patching her through to the villa where the Kings were booked. The next few seconds felt like a few decades to Blake. Alexus tightened her grip on his hand as a gruff-sounding male's voice boomed from her smartphone.

"Hello?"

"I'm calling for Carolyn King. Is she around?" "To whom am I speaking?"

Blake's heart sank to his stomach.

"This is Alexus Costilla. My son's there with his grandparents." The man paused. To Blake, it was a daunting pause. "I'm sorry...

Carolyn and Dale King are among the victims of a shooting that occurred here at Disney's Saratoga Springs Resort a short while ago."

"Oh, my God, and the kids?" Alexus exclaimed with a horrified gasp.

## *Chapter 47*

"They're fine. We found them hiding in a bedroom closet. I had an officer take them to another resort nearby. How soon can you make it here to get them?"

"I'm actually on an airplane right now, but I'll send my mom and our attorney by helicopter. Shouldn't take them more than an hour. Here, let me give you her number."

The homicide detective took an ink pen from his breast pocket and hunched over the end table to scribble down the number of his wife's favorite daytime talk show host — Rita Mae Bishop. Just knowing that he was on the phone with Alexus Costilla, the only American alive with a net worth surpassing Bill Gates', had the corpulent white Orlando Police Department detective elated.

He was 30-year-old Jim Cabenaw, and he'd never met a billionaire until now. He finished writing the number and turned to study the bodies that were still stretched out on the hardwood floor. For the umpteenth time since he'd arrived on the scene, he cast a peculiar stare at the black bandanas that were draped over the heads of Dale and Carolyn King.

"Ms. Costilla? Are you still there?" Cabenaw said into the phone. "Yes." Alexus was sobbing on the other end. "I'm here."

She sniffled audibly as Cabenaw walked over to Carolyn's body and gave the bandana a closer examination. The black bandana was covered in gold-colored, interlocking letter C's.

"You wouldn't happen to know the meaning behind this logo, would you?" asked Cabenaw. "It's two letter C's kinda hooked together like the Gucci logo. Is this some kind of clothing line logo? Seems like it may play a major role in solving this case. The logos are all over these two bandanas that were found here at the crime scene."

"Oh, my God," Alexus cried.

"God had nothing to do with this. The killers also left four dead bodyguards in the hallway, and an Asian couple across the hall where we suspect the killers waited were shot dead and — get this — beheaded. Reminds me of those drug cartels in Mexico."

King Rio

## *Chapter 48*

After four and a half hours in the sky, the private jet landed at LAX. A fleet of white Escalades were waiting on the tarmac; and forty minutes later, Blake was looking out his window at a sprawling hilltop mansion on Pacific Coast Highway in Malibu, California. He was glad his son and daughter had survived the Disney World shooting, but the loss of his parents had his heart weighed down with grief. Grief and boiling-hot anger.

He'd heard the cop telling Alexus about the bandanas the killers left at the scene of his parents' murders, and he knew what those interlocking C's stood for. Costilla Cartel. Every member of the Costilla Cartel had the double C's tattoo inked somewhere on their bodies.

Blake concluded that Jenny, Flako, Bella, or Pedro Costilla had ordered the hit on his mother and father, and he planned to kill them all just to be sure he got the right one.

"Blake and I need to be left alone for a while," Alexus said to Enrique and his men, stopping them as they were entering the massive white mansion. "Have the chefs prepare a dinner. My mom, Mercedes, Britney, and the kids are on their way here now; plane should be landing within the next two hours. And make sure we have a few SUVs waiting at O'Hare when Melonie and Tamera land in Chicago. Send them to the Trump with a million in cash."

"That cop Neal Miller isn't coming, is he?" Enrique asked.
"No. He stayed back for Patrick."

Concealed behind the dark lenses of Blake's LV sunglasses were two soul windows of hurt. He hadn't uttered a single word since the phone call on the plane. Alexus led him to an enormous, marble-floored room with an Olympic-sized swimming pool built into the middle of the floor. The indoor pool was cloaked beneath a white leather tarp, and a sofa of the same leather sat beside the pool among a row of black and gold lounge chairs.

There were two large, gold-plated handguns and a stacked row of thickly rolled cigars lying on a gold tray on the table next to the sofa.

"Have a seat, Blake," Alexus said as they made it to the sofa. "I'm sure you need a smoke. Those cigars are full of OG Kush."

Blake sat down and lit one of the cigars. He noticed that the

149

guns on the tray were .50-caliber Desert Eagles with big golden drum magazines.

He lifted one of them, cocked a round into the chamber, and set it on his lap.

"Your family just had my parents killed," Blake muttered, eying Alexus through a cloud of loud-scented smoke as she stood in front of him with her hands on her hips. "Your uncle Flako threatened my family this morning, and now they're dead. I'm killin' your uncle; him, Bella, and that fat nigga Pedro. Mercedes, too. Every mothafucka with the last name Costilla except for you and my son."

"I'm with you, Blake. Those motherfuckers can't keep trying to kill us without paying for it. They could have easily killed King Neal and Vari. I know it was Bella who sent them, because she started following Carolyn on Instagram an hour before the shooting. That's how she knew where to find them. I'm guessing she saw the Disney World pics and paid someone in Orlando or Lake Buena Vista to carry out the hit. I'm putting a hundred million dollars on her head."

"Might as well give it to me, 'cause I'm doin' it anyway." "I'll have Enrique do it personally."

"They killed my momma, killed my daddy."

"I know, Blake. Bella's gonna pay for it with her life."

Blake sucked in another mouthful of Kush smoke. The weight of the heavy handgun on his lap was just as soothing as the potent blunt. He logged into his smartphone's CNN app, saw that all the news revolved around him, and shook his head incredulously.

"T-Walk gotta die, too," he said.

"I know. But I think we should be smart about it. Let some time pass first. I say we go to Paris for a week or so. Then Rome, Greece, Spain, Egypt. Anywhere but here. Staying here in the States is far too risky with

Aunt Jenny on the loose. We can go, and I'll just leave Enrique in charge of the cartel while we're gone. He'll make sure our enemies are no longer a threat by the time we return. I'm giving Mercedes a few million to keep her out of my hair until I can figure out what to do about her."

"And T-Walk?"

150

"He will die like Young-D died." "Don't fuck wit' me, Alexus."

"I'm not playing. He'll be dead before you know it. He posted a pic on IG a few minutes ago saying he was on his way to Atlanta. Call Jeezy. Call T.I. and 2 Chains. Let them know we have a thousand bricks for T- Walk's head. Somebody'll bite."

"I will if they don't," Blake promised.

"No. You can't keep being the shooter. You're Bulletface the rapper.

You don't hear about Jay-Z and Lil Wayne shooting guns, do you? That's what you have money for. That's why you've got me. Your only job is to record music and perform it in front of millions to make even more millions. Leave everything else up to me." Alexus pointed an index finger at the table next to him. "Lift up the tray and press that button. Then step over here. I wanna show you something."

Lifting the tray, Blake found a circular gold button in the center of the white marble table. He pushed it down with the gun barrel, and then walked over to Alexus' side as the tarp covering the swimming pool began to slide open. He could not believe his eyes. The pool was at least thirty feet deep, and it was filled from end to end with cellophane-wrapped bales of hundred-dollar bills. Three rows wide, ten rows long, and stacked four bales high, the cash reached from the floor of the pool to the very top. Each bale sat on a wooden pallet.

"There's a hundred million dollars in every bale," Alexus said, stepping in front of Blake and curling her arms around him. "That's twelve billion dollars in all. My grandmother had this place built in oh-two when she couldn't fit any more money in the Matamoros vault. Had this pool customized for the sole purpose of holding her drug money. I didn't learn about it until last year when I officially became boss of the cartel. Seven of

the thirteen bedrooms are also filled with bales of cash, and there are trap doors in the gym and wine cellar that lead to even larger cash-filled rooms. Altogether, we've got about sixty-eight billion in cash stashed around this gaudy mansion, and I wanna spend every dime of it with you." She leaned in and pressed her lips to his. "I love you, Blake. We're gonna make it through this thing together. I'm the queen of the fucking world and you're my king. You're Blake King. Fucking Bulletface. Bella might have

151

thought that killing your parents would break you, but what she doesn't understand is you're a real gangster, and real gangsters don't break."

"Never," Blake agreed. Just then, Enrique appeared in the doorway... with Isabella Costilla. Her hair was wrapped around his fist, and her hands were cuffed behind her back.

"Let go of my hair, Enrique! I'm a *Costilla*! How dare you treat me this way! I had nothing to do with what happened to Blake's family."

Enrique threw her to the floor.

"You may leave," Alexus said to Enrique as she snatched the heavy gun from Blake's hand and headed toward her chubby cousin. Blake was seconds behind Alexus with the other golden Desert Eagle.

"You're no cartel boss!" Bella sneered at Alexus. She made it to her knees and spit at the two big gun barrels that were mere inches from her face. "You'll never be like Granny Costilla, or Papi. You're not even from Mexico! You're a soft-bellied American, Alexus. And you know what, Blake? Maybe I did send those guys to kill your—"

Blake pulled the trigger, and half of Bella's head departed in a viscid mist of blood, brain, and bone. Alexus followed behind him with two more

.50 caliber shots that flattened and emptied the rest of Bella's head, then Blake put another four in the belly of Bella's snow white designer dress.

## *Chapter 49*

## Four Months Later United Center, Chicago

*'It's Vice Lord till I go nigga, if ya don't know now ya know nigga*
*Up big guns let em blow nigga, murk you and all yo niggas*
*You a hoe nigga and I'm Bulletface, dat mean we ain't got shit*
*in common Tell Dr. Dre he ain't the first nigga in Hip Hop wit' a*
*billion dollas*
*Got white bricks all stacked up like winter snow in Chicago*
*Nigga diss me when the cops 'round then I'm finna blow at da*
*Five-Oh Dub Life till I die hoe, I'm a goon fuck I'm gon' lie fo'?*
*Catch you talkin' hard on front street, I'ma shoot yo' ass from*
*my side do' Cause it's Money Bagz...Management, when it's beef*
*we let da guns handle it*
*And I gangbang on that Travela shit, hang out da whip let dat*
*hammer spit...'*

His bare chest was sweaty and partially hidden behind seven white diamond chains, each necklace boasting oversized, diamond-encrusted MBM pendants with BULLETFACE written underneath them in large black diamonds. The LV bandana dangling from his front left pocket was black-and-gold and matched his belt, pants and sneakers.

Behind him on the stage was an entourage of nearly fifty men — dope boys from various Midwest cities — and before him stood a crowd of over twenty thousand Bulletface fans. Seeing them turnt up and rapping along to his songs never failed to brighten Bulletface's spirits. Right now, he was just as turnt up as they were. His adrenaline pumped fiercely. Beads of sweat rolled down his dark and determined face, and he rapped to his beat with every ounce of realness he had in him. The pain he'd experienced four months ago was still there, and it had only served to make him stronger. For as Alexus Costilla — the beautiful young billionaire who was currently waiting for him backstage — had told him just before they'd gotten even with Bella, he was Bulletface, a gangster, and gangsters don't break.

153

King Rio


To Be Continued ...
The Cocaine Princess 5
Coming Soon

Keep reading for acknowledgements and a sneak peek of Bulletface 2…

## *Acknowledgements*

My heart is with my biggest supporters: Prentice
Cassandra Kenneth Tanisha Bone Sweet Jesse Micki Georgia Hattie Yay George James Denise Dale Harrietta Shirley Harrison Sarah
George, Sr. Chanel
Mariah Shakia
Lil Rodney Bankroll Rece Hove
Roz Meach
Mama Meach Lacresha Crystal Britney Ebanee
Tasia Ashley Hunt
OG Jeff Cooper Boogie Diggs Dinero Jones Cece
Shay Rita
Khalil Amani Tysheka
Will
Johnesha Reed-Hodges
Amy Annette Gillespie Withers LaVonda Lovinglife
Sade Dobbs Yara Kaleemah
Bartholomew Edgerin Piccolo Priscilla Murray
DeShawn French Pam Williams MzNicki Ervin Tiara Mack Nikkinew Jackson Na'jara Ob
Latasha 'shine' Mack Angela Jackson
Donica NicaBoo James-Edgerton Sabrina Victorian
Ayana Knight Schawanna Morris
Jenell Gettingbacktohappy Proctor Cherrelle Colarusso
Antoinette Mitchell-Tate Diamond Maynard
Areya Wrighter-Square Michelle Sanford Harvey Kesa Muhammad
Kevin Earl Terrineka Earl Demetria Scott Aesha Carroll Jennifer White Coco J
Nika Michelle Kierra Petty Teruka Carey Shelli Marie La'Tonya West Jason Hooper Huey Sawbuck
The Whole Sicko Mobb Gang Dub Life
Melonie Frazier
Angel SouthwestCandylady Harris Lykisha Harris
Alyssa Mcbride & MizzLadii Redd

156

*Sneak Peek...*

## Bulletface 2: The Bang Bang Theory

Pint-sized "Prometh with Codeine" bottles littered the table; some empty, some full, some standing upright while others lay flat on the glass like wounded soldiers. A Ziploc bag containing close to a pound of OG Kush was also present, as well as several 50-count boxes of White Owl cigarillos, five 32-ounce bottles of Sprite, and an assortment of iPhone5 smartphones that belonged to the five rap artists who were seated on the L- shaped black leather sofa, each holding Glocks with 30-round clips and double-stacked Styrofoam cups of Lean.

Bulletface was one of them.

The other four were Young Meach, P.A.T., Will Scrill, and Yellowboy, a team of extraordinarily talented young rappers and even more extraordinary dope boys. Meach and Yellowboy were Dub Life niggas from Blake "Bulletface" King's hometown of Michigan City, Indiana. P.A.T. and Scrill were Vice Lords from Gary, Indiana. Blake had given them each $2 million in drug money on top of their $3 million for signing to his record label — Money Bagz Management — and now the five of them were on Blake's glossy black Newell tour bus, leaving an MBM concert at the United Center that had just netted Blake a cool $1 million.

"Can't believe I ain't caught that nigga T-Walk yet," Blake said, taking a tight sip of Lean and blowing Kush smoke out his nose. He briefly rested the Glock on his lap to pass Meach the blunt, then it was right back in his hand. "He think it's a game, bruh. Them niggas done shot me twelve times. They killed Lil Mike, they killed Young D, they shot Meach seven times in Miami thinkin' he was me. It's yellow tape when I see that nigga T- Walk."

"He can't hide forever," Meach said.

Will Scrill added, "We at war in the G, too. It's gon' be a hot summer for everybody this year."

Blake nodded thoughtfully. He wore Louis Vuitton from head to toe, and the large white Le Vian diamonds on his neck, wrists, and pinkies
were worth over $5 million. He was the self-proclaimed "King

157

of the Midwest", the undisputed king of the dope game, and according to the latest Forbes list, and he was also the king of Hip Hop. Often compared to Cash Money CEO Birdman, Bulletface now had an official billion-dollar net worth, a first for the Hip Hop community, and he had an unlimited reach into the billions upon billions his beautiful Black-and-Mexican girlfriend had at her disposal.

His two white iPhone5's were stacked on the table. One of them buzzed and lit up with a text from Alexus:

*'Are you gonna come and fuck me? I'm in here naked and you're out there smoking with your friends lol. Lame.'*
*'Got me fucked up,'* he replied.

Half a second later he excused himself from the gang with a quickly voiced, "Be back."

"Haaaaa," Meach laughed. "Queen A sent dat nigga a text and he went runnin'. Can't even blame you for dat, bruh."

"Aw, you awready know how I'm rockin' wit' baby," Blake proudly shouted over his shoulder.

He was already at the bedroom door. There were three bed-rooms on the tour bus — one his, one for Alexus, and the third for her bodyguards.

The door was unlocked. He pushed it open and stared in amazement at the beautiful Alexus Costilla.

Wearing only a pink wig and a pair of six-inch peep-toe Louboutin pumps, she was standing at the dresser mirror with her long black hair tied back in a ponytail, thumbing through Insta-gram on her iPhone5. She was as thick as Tahiry in the rear, and her flawless reddish-brown face, lightly veiled in makeup, drew Bulletface in like a fat kid to an ice cream truck.

Her pretty green eyes were studying him in the reflection of the mirror. She had her tongue sticking halfway out between her teeth, the tip of it seductively tracing her upper lip.

"Mind if I turn into Pinky the Pornstar for an hour or two?" Alexus asked, turning and sashaying over to where Bulletface stood at the door.

"I was wonderin' what the pink hair was about," Blake said.

158

"What do you mean? I'm Pinky. My hair's always pink."

"Yeah, a'ight. Show me." A narrow grin revealed the platinum and diamonds on Bulletface's teeth.

Alexus squatted before him and had his pants and underwear pulled down to his knees a moment later. Taking his heavy log of a penis in both hands, she squeezed and twisted at its base and gave its head a gentle kiss.

Then her head became a blur.

She began slurping his long black pole in and out of her mouth, stroking it with one hand while cradling and caressing his scrotum in the other. Her throat made squishy wet noises as she sucked in as much of his foot-long manhood as she possibly could.

Bulletface put his Glock in the shoulder-holster under his left arm and leaned back on the door, smiling contentedly.

His tour bus was enroute to the MBM after party at Adrianna's, a popular nightclub in Markham, Illinois where all the top rap artists, mobsters, pimps, and dope boys came to mingle, party, and maybe snag a bad bitch for the night. The pink-colored tour bus that was trailing behind Bulletface's, belonged to Mocha, his platinum-selling R&B artist. The three Tahoes following the pink Newell coach were full of more bodyguards.

Though he would never admit it, Bulletface was more than a little worried about the club appearance. A few weeks ago he'd released a song featuring Migos, the Atlanta rap group Chicago rapper Chief Keef was currently at odds with. Keef had conveyed his thoughts on the collaboration via Twitter:

*'How u da "king of da Midwest" and fuckin wit niggas dat don't even like us?'*

Another tweet had read:

*'Playin' both sides, dat's dat shit I'on like! War time spark broad day all night!'*

Bulletface had not taken the threat lightly, and knowing that Sosa's GBE gang was scheduled to perform tonight at Adrianna's had him feeling uneasy.

Momentarily, Alexus's tightly sucking mouth relieved him of that uneasiness.

He stepped out of his pants and underwear, then picked her up and flipped her upside down in a standing sixty-nine. He'd seen the move on a PinkyXXX porn movie. Since Alexus Costilla had suddenly decided to transform herself into Pinky, he figured it best to treat her like the porn star.

He licked and sucked her clitoris for a while, and he would have continued if the gunfire had not begun.

*****

Fredo had fifty rounds in his AK-47, and Reese had an additional fifty rounds in his Mac -11 when Ballout pulled up alongside the Bulletface tour bus in a dark-colored Explorer he'd rented from a crack-head on 64th and Normal.

As Fredo and Reese hung out the passenger's side windows and opened fire on the tour bus, all Ballout could think about was the two hundred kilograms of cocaine the GBE gang was getting for the hit on Bulletface.

The kilos were coming from a middle-aged Hispanic woman who'd contacted Sosa shortly after hearing of his burgeoning beef with Bulletface.

The woman's name was Sophia.

**Lock Down Publications and Ca$h Presents** assisted publishing packages.

### BASIC PACKAGE $499
Editing
Cover Design
Formatting

### UPGRADED PACKAGE $800
Typing
Editing
Cover Design
Formatting

### ADVANCE PACKAGE $1,200
Typing
Editing
Cover Design
Formatting
Copyright registration
Proofreading
Upload book to Amazon

### LDP SUPREME PACKAGE $1,500
Typing
Editing
Cover Design
Formatting
Copyright registration
Proofreading
Set up Amazon account
Upload book to Amazon
Advertise on LDP Amazon and Facebook page

***Other services available upon request. Additional charges
may apply
**Lock Down Publications**
**P.O. Box 944**
**Stockbridge, GA 30281-9998**
**Phone # 470 303-9761**

# Submission Guideline

Submit the first three chapters of your completed manuscript to ldpsubmissions@gmail.com, subject line: Your book's title. The manuscript must be in a .doc file and sent as an attachment. Document should be in Times New Roman, double spaced and in size 12 font. Also, provide your synopsis and full contact information. If sending multiple submissions, they must each be in a separate email.

Have a story but no way to send it electronically? You can still submit to LDP/Ca$h Presents. Send in the first three chapters, written or typed, of your completed manuscript to:

**LDP: Submissions Dept**
**Po Box 944**
**Stockbridge, Ga 30281**

*DO NOT send original manuscript. Must be a duplicate.*

Provide your synopsis and a cover letter containing your full contact information.

Thanks for considering LDP and Ca$h Presents.

## **NEW RELEASES**

KING OF THE TRENCHES 3 by GHOST & TRANAY ADAMS

JACK BOYS VS DOPE BOYS 3 by ROMELL TUKES

LIFE OF A SAVAGE 4 by ROMELL TUKES

CHI'RAQ GANGSTAS 4 by ROMELL TUKES

# King Rio

**Coming Soon from Lock Down Publications/Ca$h Presents**

BLOOD OF A BOSS **VI**

SHADOWS OF THE GAME II

TRAP BASTARD II

By **Askari**

LOYAL TO THE GAME **IV**

By **T.J. & Jelissa**

TRUE SAVAGE **VIII**

MIDNIGHT CARTEL IV

DOPE BOY MAGIC IV

CITY OF KINGZ III

NIGHTMARE ON SILENT AVE II

THE PLUG OF LIL MEXICO II

CLASSIC CITY II

By **Chris Green**

BLAST FOR ME **III**

A SAVAGE DOPEBOY III

CUTTHROAT MAFIA III

DUFFLE BAG CARTEL VII

HEARTLESS GOON VI

By **Ghost**

A HUSTLER'S DECEIT III

KILL ZONE II

BAE BELONGS TO ME III

TIL DEATH II

By **Aryanna**

KING OF THE TRAP III

By **T.J. Edwards**

GORILLAZ IN THE BAY V

3X KRAZY III

STRAIGHT BEAST MODE III

164

**De'Kari**
KINGPIN KILLAZ IV
STREET KINGS III
PAID IN BLOOD III
CARTEL KILLAZ IV
DOPE GODS III
**Hood Rich**
SINS OF A HUSTLA II
**ASAD**
RICH $AVAGE III
**By Martell Troublesome Bolden**
YAYO V
Bred In The Game 2
**S. Allen**
THE STREETS WILL TALK II
**By Yolanda Moore**
SON OF A DOPE FIEND III
HEAVEN GOT A GHETTO II
SKI MASK MONEY II
**By Renta**
LOYALTY AIN'T PROMISED III
**By Keith Williams**
I'M NOTHING WITHOUT HIS LOVE II
SINS OF A THUG II
TO THE THUG I LOVED BEFORE II
IN A HUSTLER I TRUST II
**By Monet Dragun**
QUIET MONEY IV
EXTENDED CLIP III
THUG LIFE IV
By **Trai'Quan**
THE STREETS MADE ME IV

# King Rio

By **Larry D. Wright**
IF YOU CROSS ME ONCE II
ANGEL IV
By **Anthony Fields**
THE STREETS WILL NEVER CLOSE IV
By **K'ajji**
HARD AND RUTHLESS III
KILLA KOUNTY III
By **Khufu**
MONEY GAME III
By **Smoove Dolla**
JACK BOYS VS DOPE BOYS IV
A GANGSTA'S QUR'AN V
COKE GIRLZ II
COKE BOYS II
LIFE OF A SAVAGE V
CHI'RAQ GANGSTAS V
By **Romell Tukes**
MURDA WAS THE CASE III
**Elijah R. Freeman**
THE STREETS NEVER LET GO III
By **Robert Baptiste**
AN UNFORESEEN LOVE IV
By **Meesha**

MONEY MAFIA II
By **Jibril Williams**
QUEEN OF THE ZOO III
By **Black Migo**
VICIOUS LOYALTY III
By **Kingpen**

A GANGSTA'S PAIN III
**By J-Blunt**
CONFESSIONS OF A JACKBOY III
**By Nicholas Lock**
GRIMEY WAYS III
**By Ray Vinci**
KING KILLA II
**By Vincent "Vitto" Holloway**
BETRAYAL OF A THUG II
**By Fre$h**
THE MURDER QUEENS III
**By Michael Gallon**
THE BIRTH OF A GANGSTER III
**By Delmont Player**
TREAL LOVE II
**By Le'Monica Jackson**
FOR THE LOVE OF BLOOD II
**By Jamel Mitchell**
RAN OFF ON DA PLUG II
**By Paper Boi Rari**
HOOD CONSIGLIERE II
**By Keese**
PRETTY GIRLS DO NASTY THINGS II
**By Nicole Goosby**
PROTÉGÉ OF A LEGEND II
**By Corey Robinson**
IT'S JUST ME AND YOU II
**By Ah'Million**
BORN IN THE GRAVE II
**By Self Made Tay**
FOREVER GANGSTA III
**By Adrian Dulan**

King Rio

GORILLAZ IN THE TRENCHES II
**By SayNoMore**

**Available Now**

RESTRAINING ORDER **I & II**
By **CA$H & Coffee**
LOVE KNOWS NO BOUNDARIES **I II & III**
By **Coffee**
RAISED AS A GOON I, II,  III & IV
BRED BY THE SLUMS I, II, III
BLAST FOR ME I & II
ROTTEN TO THE CORE I II III
A BRONX TALE I, II, III
DUFFLE BAG CARTEL I II III IV V VI
HEARTLESS GOON I II III IV V
A SAVAGE DOPEBOY I II
DRUG LORDS I II III
CUTTHROAT MAFIA I II
KING OF THE TRENCHES
By **Ghost**
LAY IT DOWN **I & II**
LAST OF A DYING BREED I II
BLOOD STAINS OF A SHOTTA I & II III
By **Jamaica**

168

LOYAL TO THE GAME I II III

LIFE OF SIN I, II III

By **TJ & Jelissa**

BLOODY COMMAS I & II

SKI MASK CARTEL I  II & III

KING OF NEW YORK I II,III IV V

RISE TO POWER I II III

COKE KINGS I II III IV V

BORN HEARTLESS I II III IV

KING OF THE TRAP I II

By **T.J. Edwards**

IF LOVING HIM IS WRONG…I & II

LOVE ME EVEN WHEN IT HURTS I II III

By **Jelissa**

WHEN THE STREETS CLAP BACK I & II III

THE HEART OF A SAVAGE I II III IV

MONEY MAFIA

LOYAL TO THE SOIL I II III

By **Jibril Williams**

A DISTINGUISHED THUG STOLE MY HEART I II & III

LOVE SHOULDN'T HURT I II III IV

RENEGADE BOYS I II III IV

PAID IN KARMA I II III

SAVAGE STORMS I II III

AN UNFORESEEN LOVE I II III

By **Meesha**

A GANGSTER'S CODE I &, II III

A GANGSTER'S SYN I II III

THE SAVAGE LIFE I II III

CHAINED TO THE STREETS I II III

BLOOD ON THE MONEY I II III

A GANGSTA'S PAIN I II

# King Rio

**By J-Blunt**
PUSH IT TO THE LIMIT
By **Bre' Hayes**
BLOOD OF A BOSS **I, II, III,  IV, V**
SHADOWS OF THE GAME
TRAP BASTARD
By **Askari**
THE STREETS BLEED MURDER **I, II & III**
THE HEART OF A GANGSTA I II& III
By **Jerry Jackson**
CUM FOR ME I II III IV V VI VII VIII
An **LDP Erotica Collaboration**
BRIDE OF A HUSTLA **I  II & II**
THE FETTI GIRLS **I, II& III**
CORRUPTED BY A GANGSTA I, II III, IV
BLINDED BY HIS LOVE
THE PRICE YOU PAY FOR LOVE I, II ,III
DOPE GIRL MAGIC I II III
By **Destiny Skai**
WHEN A GOOD GIRL GOES BAD
By **Adrienne**
THE COST OF LOYALTY I II III
**By Kweli**
A GANGSTER'S REVENGE **I II III & IV**
THE BOSS MAN'S DAUGHTERS I II III IV V
A SAVAGE LOVE  **I & II**
BAE BELONGS TO ME I II
A HUSTLER'S DECEIT I, II, III
WHAT BAD BITCHES DO I, II, III
SOUL OF A MONSTER I II III
KILL ZONE

170

A DOPE BOY'S QUEEN I II III

TIL DEATH

By **Aryanna**

A KINGPIN'S AMBITON

A KINGPIN'S AMBITION **II**

I MURDER FOR THE DOUGH

By **Ambitious**

TRUE SAVAGE I II III IV V VI VII

DOPE BOY MAGIC I, II, III

MIDNIGHT CARTEL I II III

CITY OF KINGZ I II

NIGHTMARE ON SILENT AVE

THE PLUG OF LIL MEXICO II

CLASSIC CITY

By **Chris Green**

A DOPEBOY'S PRAYER

By **Eddie "Wolf" Lee**

THE KING CARTEL **I, II & III**

By **Frank Gresham**

THESE NIGGAS AIN'T LOYAL **I, II & III**

By **Nikki Tee**

GANGSTA SHYT **I II &III**

By **CATO**

THE ULTIMATE BETRAYAL

By **Phoenix**

BOSS'N UP **I , II & III**

By **Royal Nicole**

I LOVE YOU TO DEATH

By **Destiny J**

I RIDE FOR MY HITTA

I STILL RIDE FOR MY HITTA

By **Misty Holt**

# King Rio

LOVE & CHASIN' PAPER
By **Qay Crockett**
TO DIE IN VAIN
SINS OF A HUSTLA
By **ASAD**
BROOKLYN HUSTLAZ
By **Boogsy Morina**
BROOKLYN ON LOCK I & II
By **Sonovia**
GANGSTA CITY
By **Teddy Duke**
A DRUG KING AND HIS DIAMOND I & II III
A DOPEMAN'S RICHES
HER MAN, MINE'S TOO I, II
CASH MONEY HO'S
THE WIFEY I USED TO BE I II
PRETTY GIRLS DO NASTY THINGS
**By Nicole Goosby**
TRAPHOUSE KING **I II & III**
KINGPIN KILLAZ I II III
STREET KINGS I II
PAID IN BLOOD **I II**
CARTEL KILLAZ I II III
DOPE GODS I II
By **Hood Rich**
LIPSTICK KILLAH **I, II, III**
CRIME OF PASSION I II & III
FRIEND OR FOE I II III
By **Mimi**
STEADY MOBBN' **I, II, III**
THE STREETS STAINED MY SOUL I II III

The Cocaine Princess 4

By **Marcellus Allen**

WHO SHOT YA **I, II, III**

SON OF A DOPE FIEND I II

HEAVEN GOT A GHETTO

SKI MASK MONEY

**Renta**

GORILLAZ IN THE BAY **I II III IV**

TEARS OF A GANGSTA I II

3X KRAZY I II

STRAIGHT BEAST MODE I II

**DE'KARI**

TRIGGADALE I II III

MURDAROBER WAS THE CASE I II

**Elijah R. Freeman**

GOD BLESS THE TRAPPERS I, II, III

THESE SCANDALOUS STREETS I, II, III

FEAR MY GANGSTA I, II, III IV, V

THESE STREETS DON'T LOVE NOBODY I, II

BURY ME A G I, II, III, IV, V

A GANGSTA'S EMPIRE I, II, III, IV

THE DOPEMAN'S BODYGAURD I II

THE REALEST KILLAZ I II III

THE LAST OF THE OGS I II III

**Tranay Adams**

THE STREETS ARE CALLING

**Duquie Wilson**

MARRIED TO A BOSS I II III

**By Destiny Skai & Chris Green**

KINGZ OF THE GAME I II III IV V VI

**Playa Ray**

SLAUGHTER GANG I II III

RUTHLESS HEART I II III

173

# King Rio

**By Willie Slaughter**

FUK SHYT

**By Blakk Diamond**

DON'T F#CK WITH MY HEART I II

**By Linnea**

ADDICTED TO THE DRAMA I II III

IN THE ARM OF HIS BOSS II

**By Jamila**

YAYO I II III IV

A SHOOTER'S AMBITION I II

BRED IN THE GAME

**By S. Allen**

TRAP GOD  I II III

RICH $AVAGE I II

MONEY IN THE GRAVE I II III

**By Martell Troublesome Bolden**

FOREVER GANGSTA I II

GLOCKS ON SATIN SHEETS I II

**By Adrian Dulan**

TOE TAGZ I II III IV

LEVELS TO THIS SHYT I II

IT'S JUST ME AND YOU

**By Ah'Million**

KINGPIN DREAMS  I II III

RAN OFF ON DA PLUG

**By Paper Boi Rari**

CONFESSIONS OF A GANGSTA I II III IV

CONFESSIONS OF A JACKBOY I II

**By Nicholas Lock**

I'M NOTHING WITHOUT HIS LOVE

SINS OF A THUG

174

The Cocaine Princess 4

TO THE THUG I LOVED BEFORE

A GANGSTA SAVED XMAS

IN A HUSTLER I TRUST

**By Monet Dragun**

CAUGHT UP IN THE LIFE I II III

THE STREETS NEVER LET GO I II

**By Robert Baptiste**

NEW TO THE GAME I II III

MONEY, MURDER & MEMORIES I II III

By **Malik D. Rice**

LIFE OF A SAVAGE I II III IV

A GANGSTA'S QUR'AN I II III IV

MURDA SEASON I II III

GANGLAND CARTEL I II III

CHI'RAQ GANGSTAS I II III IV

KILLERS ON ELM STREET I II III

JACK BOYZ N DA BRONX I II III

A DOPEBOY'S DREAM I II III

JACK BOYS VS DOPE BOYS I II III

COKE GIRLZ

COKE BOYS

**By Romell Tukes**

LOYALTY AIN'T PROMISED I II

**By Keith Williams**

QUIET MONEY I II III

THUG LIFE I II III

EXTENDED CLIP I II

A GANGSTA'S PARADISE

By **Trai'Quan**

THE STREETS MADE ME I II III

By **Larry D. Wright**

THE ULTIMATE SACRIFICE I, II, III, IV, V, VI

King Rio

KHADIFI
IF YOU CROSS ME ONCE
ANGEL I II III
IN THE BLINK OF AN EYE
By **Anthony Fields**
THE LIFE OF A HOOD STAR
By **Ca$h & Rashia Wilson**
THE STREETS WILL NEVER CLOSE I II III
By **K'ajji**
CREAM I II III
THE STREETS WILL TALK
By **Yolanda Moore**
NIGHTMARES OF A HUSTLA I II III
By **King Dream**
CONCRETE KILLA I II III
VICIOUS LOYALTY I II
By **Kingpen**
HARD AND RUTHLESS I II
MOB TOWN 251
THE BILLIONAIRE BENTLEYS I II III
By **Von Diesel**
GHOST MOB
**Stilloan Robinson**
MOB TIES I II III IV V VI
SOUL OF A HUSTLER, HEART OF A KILLER
GORILLAZ IN THE TRENCHES
By **SayNoMore**
BODYMORE MURDERLAND I II III
THE BIRTH OF A GANGSTER I II
By **Delmont Player**
FOR THE LOVE OF A BOSS

176

**By C. D. Blue**
MOBBED UP I II III IV
THE BRICK MAN I II III IV
THE COCAINE PRINCESS I II III IV V
**By King Rio**
KILLA KOUNTY I II III
**By Khufu**
MONEY GAME I II
**By Smoove Dolla**
A GANGSTA'S KARMA I II
**By FLAME**
KING OF THE TRENCHES I II III
by **GHOST & TRANAY ADAMS**
QUEEN OF THE ZOO I II
By **Black Migo**
GRIMEY WAYS I II
**By Ray Vinci**
XMAS WITH AN ATL SHOOTER
**By Ca$h & Destiny Skai**
KING KILLA
**By Vincent "Vitto" Holloway**
BETRAYAL OF A THUG
**By Fre$h**
THE MURDER QUEENS I II
**By Michael Gallon**
TREAL LOVE
**By Le'Monica Jackson**
FOR THE LOVE OF BLOOD
**By Jamel Mitchell**
HOOD CONSIGLIERE
**By Keese**
PROTÉGÉ OF A LEGEND

# King Rio

**By Corey Robinson**
**BORN IN THE GRAVE**
**By Self Made Tay**
**MOAN IN MY MOUTH**
**By XTASY**

**<u>BOOKS BY LDP'S CEO, CA$H</u>**

TRUST IN NO MAN

TRUST IN NO MAN 2

TRUST IN NO MAN 3

BONDED BY BLOOD

SHORTY GOT A THUG

THUGS CRY

THUGS CRY 2

THUGS CRY 3

TRUST NO BITCH

TRUST NO BITCH 2

TRUST NO BITCH 3

TIL MY CASKET DROPS

RESTRAINING ORDER

RESTRAINING ORDER 2

IN LOVE WITH A CONVICT

LIFE OF A HOOD STAR

XMAS WITH AN ATL SHOOTER